BLACK AND BLUE
AN AUTUMN FROST STORY

JESSE FRESCO

Edited by Brian Paone
Interior Formatting by Kari Holloway
Cover Artwork and Formatting by Amy Hunter
Autumn Frost Cover Model: Tiffanie Marie Ford

"Have you ever noticed when you're driving that anyone who's driving slower than you is an idiot? And anyone driving faster than you is a maniac?"

— George Carlin

Chapter One

He ran.

Fast as he could, he ran. His sneakers pounded the pavement. His left foot nearly slipped from its hold as the laces had come undone. Sweat drenched his face, his shirt, his crotch. Cobwebs of powerlines draped from rooftop to rooftop as he rounded a corner into a grungy, filthy alleyway, with cracked misshapen concrete. The stench from multiple piles of rotting trash ran rampant in the Baltimore spring heat. He ignored the trash and kept running, fast as he could, because his mother had told him to.

Twenty minutes earlier, he was just a fifteen-year-old kid named Mateo. He was three-quarters Hispanic and had lived in Baltimore all his life with his mother and father, Juliana and Marcus. His mother was full Hispanic from Argentina; his father was half-Hispanic and from Baltimore. Unlike most of the Hispanic residents in Baltimore's West Brooklyn or East Patterson Park, Mateo's family lived reasonably well in the trendy, vibrant, and family friendly Canton area near the waterfront. Mateo loved his home, and he loved Baltimore.

At that moment, though, he didn't love it. He was terrified of it.

He kept running, fast as he could. Because they had taken her.

Mateo rounded another corner and emerged onto South Ellwood Avenue. He swiveled his head left, then right, then left again. He saw no one, just the occasional car passing farther down the street. He breathed hard and hunched over, leaning on his knees to get some air into his lungs. The wretched trash-strewn air finally hit him, but he didn't care.

As he sucked in putrid air, he noticed his untied shoelace. He kneeled, coughed, and retied it.

Five seconds later, a pair of black Chevy Tahoes zipped around the corners of South Ellwood—one on the south side, one on the north, which violated traffic laws, as South Ellwood was a one-way street.

A fresh rush of adrenaline pumped through Mateo's veins as he darted across the street and toward another alleyway. Large men wearing black shirts, jeans, masks, Kevlar vests, and sunglasses dashed from the vehicles. All brandished high-caliber assault rifles.

Four of the masked men gave chase, their kits clicking and clacking with every step. "Go, go, go," one yelled. "Get the fucking spic!"

Several of them flipped off their safeties, ready for action.

Mateo pushed through the pain of exhaustion. His chest hurt, his legs hurt, everything hurt. But he kept going.

***

Twenty minutes earlier, he and his mother ran errands in Fells Point. The farmers' market was having a sale on freshly stocked fruits and vegetables. Mateo and his mother walked from Canton to the market—almost a straight line. It was a beautiful sunny day, no reason to not enjoy it. Mateo mainly tagged along because he wanted to visit The Sound Garden, a record store on Thames Street. He would help her with groceries, then he could buy a new album.

After they purchased their groceries, and Mateo purchased a new music album which his mother had recommended—*Bad is Beautiful* by Ralph Convert and The Bad Examples—they began the straight line walk home.

Ten minutes from their rowhouse, a pair of black Chevy Tahoes screeched to a halt, and armed men wearing masks burst forth from all the doors and aimed their automatic rifles at them. Mateo and Juliana froze and raised their hands, terrified. The masked men rushed forward, grabbed Juliana's arms, and threw her to the ground. As the bags fell from her hands, fresh apples and carrots scattered across the pavement. One masked man grabbed Mateo from behind and dragged him toward one of the vehicles. The record fell from Mateo's grip and landed on its edge, possibly damaging it. There was screaming, yelling, crying.

No one intervened. A small crowd had gathered, but, instead of helping, they recorded the incident on their cellphones.

As she was on the ground, Mateo's mother screamed out, "Mateo, run now! Run! Don't stop running!"

With all his might, Mateo thrashed about, throwing the masked assailant off balance. The pair toppled over and landed on the pavement with a loud *thud*.

As the assailant pulled Juliana to her feet, she screamed again, "*Run!*"

Mateo eyed his would-be kidnapper and saw the government logo imprinted on his vest. *Oh no.*

In a panic, he obeyed. And ran.

***

Autumn smirked and asked over the phone, "And what are you wearing right now?"

"Oh, I bet you'd love to know, wouldn't you?" Becky answered on the other end of the call.

"I would, actually." Autumn leaned back in her driver's seat, running her fingers across her clavicle.

"Well, you'll just have to come by tonight to find out, won't you?"

"Hehe, you tease."

"You love it."

"Yeah, I do. Love you, babe."

"Love you too. See you tonight."

Autumn Frost hung up and looked out her driver's side window. She was parked on South Clinton Street, a one-way road in Canton. A four-way intersection lay just ahead of her parking space, which connected Clinton to Hudson Street. The sun shone, and a light breeze cut though the warmer-than-normal springtime temperature. Even so, she would take the heat over the bitter cold of winter.

Feeling cramped from her long drive, she opened the door and stepped into the open air. She had just endured a ninety-minute drive from Annapolis to Baltimore. She typically wouldn't drive that far north, as she was based in the Annapolis area, but this instance had been a special case. As a TAF (To-and-From) driver, it was rare for a client to ask to drive from one major city to another, but it did happen on occasion. The ride request had been from an elderly couple who wanted to head north to visit family in the Canton area. It was a hefty fee, but the couple was very well off financially, so they didn't mind the rate.

And so, they had paid Autumn rather handsomely to drive north to Baltimore. As her luck would have it, a car accident on Route 97 North had caused a thirty-minute delay, which upped the drive time to ninety minutes. The elderly couple hadn't complained though and enjoyed Autumn's company on the snails crawl forward on 97.

With the drop off complete, Autumn had considered her options: head back toward Annapolis or pick up rides in Baltimore. She knew the town well enough, and GPS alleviated much of the hassle of direction, but it was still a town with its own quirks. Roads were typically in poorer condition than Annapolis, many streets were one-way, traffic near the harbor was almost constant, and the town itself was divided into various boroughs, distinguished by class and race. It was, in many ways, like a miniature version of New York City, which made it both beautiful and dangerous at the same time.

Autumn opened the TAF app and checked today's income. Due to the drive north, she was close to her daily goal and decided to take a break. In the hot Baltimore air, she stretched her arms. As she arched her back, her shoulders and spine cracked. Her red hair caught the breeze and shimmered brightly in the sunlight. She wore a deep-green tank top and black jeans. The long pants were mainly because she despised wearing shorts. During the hotter seasons, perspiration stains would show through any light clothing, and her legs would soak into the fabric of her car seat. Darker attire and long pants were needed to hide the ass sweat.

A horn honked down the street as a gang of kids on bikes blazed through an intersection. They paid no attention to the screaming and honking and continued on their way.

Autumn walked toward Ellie's Tavern. According to her maps, this was one of multiple taverns within a three-mile radius. *God, is this part of Baltimore nothing but bars?* After a moment's consideration, she realized it wasn't that much different from Annapolis—a bar almost every block. She shrugged off the thought and opened the door.

The air conditioning blasted her face from the clean yet rustic interior, like being inside a brick oven that had just received a good once-over. The narrow building featured a long wooden walkway stretching to the opposite side of the room. Unlit strings of Christmas lights zigzagged across the rafters. The bar itself was wooden and polished to a sheen. Cone-shaped lights hung over the bar and shone onto the bar top. High-top tables stood under each of the windows, providing a decent view of the street outside. A smell of fried seafood hung in the air, which was exactly what Autumn craved.

She snatched a seat at the bar and reached over the counter to grab a menu.

The large and bearded bartender said, "How's it going? Welcome to Ellie's. My name's Mike. What can I get for you?"

Autumn perused the menu. "Could I get a club soda and an order of fried calamari, please?"

"Sure thing. Coming right up." Mike stepped away to prepare Autumn's drink.

As she waited, Autumn spotted a set of large photo prints of Baltimore-specific locations on the wall behind her: the Baltimore port, Camden Yards, the Domino Sugar factory across the harbor. Ellie's felt like a slightly classier place than Annapolis's Stan and Joe's Tavern, which itself felt more like a dive. Ellie's had a much cleaner appeal, more in line with modern gentrification. Despite that, Autumn felt comfortable in the atmosphere, and, if nothing else, it was much cooler inside there than outside in the blasting sun.

Autumn's drink arrived, and she took a long sip, held back a burp, and checked the socials on her phone. A few minutes later, the bartender slid Autumn's meal in front of her: fried calamari, with a side of french fries and celery. She savored every bite; it had been a long time since she had had any kind of seafood—a true crime for a Marylander. The calamari were good but not great. Even so, she ordered a to-go plate for her girlfriend, Becky. It would be a nice surprise for her once she got home from work at the hospital.

"How is it?" Mike asked her.

"Pretty good. Had better though. No offense."

"It's a bit out of season, I think."

"Probably the reason."

"First time in here?"

"Yeah. Up here for work. Gonna head back to Annapolis after this."

"Oh, Naptown. You like it better down there?"

"I grew up there, so it's home turf. Baltimore has its nice spots though. Did a bar crawl through Canton years ago."

"I think there's a bar crawl every other weekend here. Nothing but stumbling drunks as far as the eye can see. Though today is the Baltimore Pride Parade. Pretty sure that's where most people will be starting out."

"Oh, shit! I should probably head out before the traffic starts."

"Probably a good idea."

Autumn paid her tab, thanked Mike, snatched the to-go bag of Becky's dinner, and headed out. As she approached her car, she double tapped the Unlock button. She opened the rear driver's side door and set the bag on the floor. As she slid into her driver's seat, she checked her phone. No messages. While she could keep picking up rides in town, Autumn wasn't interested in doing more TAF runs through Baltimore, especially if a parade would disrupt traffic. She set her phone on her dashboard holder and set her GPS destination for Annapolis. Once she reached Route 97 South, she could figure it out just fine from there.

A loud bang sounded on the rear driver's side door. Autumn twisted to looked out the back, thinking one of the bike-riding kids may have hit her. She saw a young Hispanic teen, panting and out of breath.

He hurriedly wrenched open the door, slid into the back seat, then slammed and locked the door.

"What the *fuck*? Get outta my car," Autumn screamed.

"Please help! You need to drive!"

"Get outta my car!"

"Please! They're chasing me!"

Autumn shifted her gaze upward and saw four large men in vests and masks running toward the car. One raised an assault rifle and took aim. He screamed something indiscernible.

"Oh shit!" Autumn turned over the engine, shifted into gear, and bolted away, nearly swerving into a car as she merged onto the road.

The other car veered away and stopped just before hitting a worn-down telephone pole. The near impact cut off the armed men, forcing them to lower their rifles. Autumn sped toward the intersection of Clinton and Hudson, then noticed the red light. She cut hard right and joined the traffic on Hudson Street, heading east.

The masked men walked into the middle of the street as the pair of Chevy Tahoes screeched to a stop. The rear doors opened, and the men climbed in.

Autumn pressed hard on the accelerator, desperate to escape. "There better be a good fucking explanation!"

"They took my mom. She told me to run away. I didn't know where to go that they wouldn't find me."

"If this is a gang thing, I'll drop you off after a few blocks. You can call the cops on your own."

The kid leaned forward and grasped the back of the passenger seat. "No, you can't!"

"Why not?"

"Because they're not cops! They're ICE!"

Autumn paused, her mouth agape. After a beat, she turned around and screamed, "Are you fucking kidding me?"

Chapter Two

utumn's Honda Accord surged down Hudson Street—a two-lane road flanked on both sides by parked cars and trees in equidistant increments of twenty feet—with blistering speed. Thankfully, the city properly maintained the road itself—not a pothole in sight. Unfortunately, every intersection was home to a stop light, which meant rolling the dice whether she would get a green, yellow, or red as she and her new passenger blazed down the street.

As she crossed the next four-way intersection, which was mercifully green, she saw two large black Tahoes giving chase in her rearview mirror. She cursed to herself and buckled her seatbelt.

"This is just how I wanted to spend my afternoon," Autumn said sarcastically "You, whatever your name is, sit back and buckle up."

The kid sat back on the passenger side and buckled his seatbelt. Beads of sweat rolled down his face onto his blue Judas Priest T-shirt. "My name's Mateo."

"Well, Mateo, you just ruined my day, good and thoroughly. Thanks for that."

The car raced through the next intersection; a green shifted to yellow as they passed through. A bad sign. All stop lights in each area tended to change as a unit to maintain proper traffic flow, which meant somewhere ahead one of them would shift to red before they made it through.

Traffic became congested. Autumn was forced to slow down as a large Cadillac DeVille that had seen better days meandered down the road without a care in the world. Autumn slowed to 25 mph and slammed on her horn. *Honk! Honk! Honk!* "Get outta the way!"

The Cadillac driver stuck his hand out the window and flipped her the middle finger.

"Yeah, fuck you too!"

The Tahoes gained distance to only three car lengths from the Accord. Autumn craned her head around and saw them still gaining. One merged into the oncoming lane to get alongside her to PIT her vehicle.

"Whatever you did, kid, really pissed them off."

"I didn't do anything. I was just out—"

"One sec." Autumn, desperate to gain distance and get around the Cadillac, swerved left into the oncoming lane. She gunned the engine and passed the Cadillac.

The driver screamed obscenities and told her to get off the road.

She darted back into the proper lane ahead of the Cadillac and, just for the hell of it, gave him that ginger *thank you* wave that drivers exchange while passing on the highway. The Accord crossed the next intersection as a yellow light turned red. Not good.

"What were you saying, kid?" Autumn quickly wiped sweat from her brow.

"I was out with my mom getting groceries. They just pulled up and grabbed us. We didn't do anything."

"Where's your mom now?"

"I don't know. They took her."

"Fuck. These fucking guys. Fucking ICE!"

Established just after 9/11, under the Department of Homeland Security, the Immigration and Customs Enforcement organization had worked within the bounds and confines of the law to arrest and deport individuals who had violated immigration regulations or had expired green cards, all in the name of national security. However, the presidential reelect of Donald Trump repurposed the organization from an immigration enforcement detail to a heavily armed Gestapo-type military unit. The second-term administration encouraged many trainees, and even trained them, to violate all civil rights and to ignore Constitutional law. Instead of bringing order and security to the nation, they had become the biggest bullies in America—a highly volatile renegade faction with itchy trigger fingers, and they were desperate to scratch them.

Finally, it happened. A red light.

"Goddammit!" Autumn slammed the gas pedal to the floorboard and went for it, narrowly avoiding a crossing vehicle. The Accord emerged from the intersection unscathed. Blind luck.

The dense passing traffic forced the Tahoes to decelerate and swerve into an awkward stop. The

Tahoes stood diagonally in the street as they waited for the light to change.

Farther down the street, Autumn's Accord rolled onward. She exhaled sharply from holding her breath through the intersection. With her body catching up to her brain, she watched the Tahoes in her mirror, still parked and waiting for the light to change. She had to get off Hudson Street ASAP.

"How well do you know this neighborhood?" Autumn asked Mateo. She saw him in the rearview mirror clenching the seat in terror.

"I don't live far away. I know it pretty well." He gulped hard.

"Is there anywhere we can hide till they go away?"

"Keep going straight, then turn right. That'll take you to Haven Street. Then turn left to go under the highway on O'Donnell. There's a bunch of abandoned warehouses everywhere over there."

Autumn slowed to a stop at another red light. She anxiously tapped her fingers on the steering wheel while glancing in the rearview mirror every few seconds. "Come on, come on, come on!" She glanced again and saw the beastly vehicles passing through the intersection toward her. "Oh shit! Come on!"

At the last second, the light turned green. Autumn slammed on the gas pedal and sped through the intersection, her tires peeling out. She swerved right, narrowly avoiding one of the Tahoes attempting to PIT her again. The Tahoe regained control and continued the chase.

Bobbing, weaving, dodging incoming attacks, Autumn finally reached the three-way intersection for Haven Street. The one advantage Autumn's Accord had over the two Chevy Tahoes was maneuverability. As she was lower to the ground, her turning radius was sharper and could accelerate much faster. Tahoes had power, but they sacrificed all other driving capabilities in favor of that power. Brute force meant nothing if it couldn't be aimed correctly.

Autumn grasped the handbrake at her right thigh. "Let's see if you can do this, you Nazi pricks." She pulled on the handbrake and turned hard right. The tires screamed in protest as the Accord spun ninety degrees, becoming parallel with Haven Street. She released the brake, pushed hard on the accelerator, and dashed forward, just barely missing the front bumper of one of the pursuing trucks.

The two Tahoes barreled through the intersection, unable to turn as sharp as the Accord. In unison, they mounted the curb on the opposite side of the street, swerved out of control for a split second, then righted their course after Autumn and Mateo.

By the time the two vehicles had dismounted the curb and reentered traffic, Autumn's Accord had already turned left onto O'Donnell Street, escaping their sight.

***

Autumn had to let off the gas as she soared down the road. O'Donnell Street, which ran parallel to an overpass highway, was all torn up and in extreme disrepair. Potholes, manhole covers, and small concrete berms, which had elevated from the roadway due to time and erosion, pockmarked both sides of the road. On the right side of the road was a drab and brown abandoned two-story boarded-up building with no personality whatsoever. Autumn vaguely wondered what it had been used for. Textiles, car parts—who knew? It was also completely fenced off, which made it a no-go for hiding. The opposite side of the road featured a large open concrete lot filled with mounds of city trash. Scrap metal, rotting wooden boards, the occasional abandoned vehicle. And just behind the heaps of garbage sat a large red brick building, with smashed-out windows and a loading bay door large enough for a truck to fit inside. No fence surrounded the building either.

Perfect.

"You doing okay, Mateo?" Autumn asked.

"Yeah, I'm okay. You're a really good driver."

"Yeah, because I'm not great at much else. Hang on." Autumn turned sharp left onto South Kresson Street. The unmarked road led to a factory district of nondescript brick buildings. Opposite the derelict warehouse was a smattering of random vehicles parked outside a newly occupied building, workers on the job for the day. As the Accord arced wide around the empty warehouse, Autumn scanned the building for an open entrance. She located a busted open bay door on the back side that some larger vehicle had plowed through, more than likely an accident from years prior. She slowed and approached cautiously, wary of security cameras and armed guards. While they probably wouldn't arrest her, any kind of security would surely force her off the property, which, given the circumstances, was not an option.

Autumn eased the Accord through the gap into the musty rundown interior, where gigantic metal crushers, broken-down hydraulic presses, and enormous shredders were caked in dust, grime, and refuse. A plethora of graffiti vandalized the walls—some new, while some decades old. A pair of giant Baltimore rats scurried away as the Accord entered. The front of the building contained a concrete ramp, flanked by faded yellow handrails that led to a trio of loading bay doors for tractor trailers. One door remained three-quarters open, allowing a long shaft of golden light to spill across the dirt-ridden floor. Autumn finally realized the building was a recycling mill, long since abandoned. It was cheaper to leave it up and let it rot than for the city to tear it down and build something new.

To avoid anyone seeing them through the busted open door, Autumn pulled right, then backed into a tight dividing space between the shredder and the hydraulic press. It was so tight that they would barely be able to open the Accord doors halfway. She set the parking brake and killed the engine. Once the sound dissipated, it was eerily quiet inside the building, save for the *tink tink tink* of the cooling engine.

Autumn unbuckled her seatbelt and twisted herself around to look at the scared kid in the backseat, a hint of anger flickering in her eyes. "All right, be straight with me. My name is Autumn, and I was having a very good day before I met you, Mateo.

There's gotta be a reason these dicks are after you. There's always a reason."

"There's nothing. I didn't do anything. They just … showed up." Mateo's breath staggered, as he was on the verge of crying.

"Take me through it, step by step, till you jumped into my car."

Tears fell from his eyes, but he managed to go through the day's events well enough for Autumn to get the gist of what had happened. Even after hearing it, it still didn't quite add up.

"So, they were just profiling you and your mom? How did they know where you were if it was just profiling?"

"I don't know."

Disheartened and confused, Autumn turned around in her seat and stared out the windshield. The pair of rats had returned and ran across the yellowed handrails. "Something doesn't add up. Do you have a phone?"

Wiping away tears, Mateo pulled a cellphone from his pants pocket. "Yeah, right here."

"Anyone you can call?"

"My dad. But why not the police?"

"Do you really trust the police to not turn you over to ICE?"

After a moment's consideration, Mateo shrugged, accepting that Autumn was correct. Police, even in blue states, had been known to work alongside ICE agents and, in many instances, protect them during raids and arrests. All figures of authority were suspected in their allegiance in Trump's America.

"You know what? Give me your dad's number. I'll call him from here. Probably safer. They might be tracing your cellphone. We need to check to see if they got him too."

"I don't think they would get him."

"Why's that?"

"He's half-White, and from Baltimore."

"Eh, lucky him, I guess."

Mateo sniffled and wiped away a stream of snot with his hand. Autumn retrieved a wad of soft tissues from the glovebox. She handed them backward without looking. Mateo accepted them and blew his nose.

Autumn sighed and rubbed her eyes. The dust from the building somehow found its way inside the car and irritated her. "All right, we're gonna just wait here for a bit till they give up, then I'll take you home to your dad. You live close by?"

"Yeah, not far."

"Good, because I'm trying to save on gas."

***

"You got the dash cam footage?" Silten asked.

"Yeah, going through it now," McDonald responded. As the Tahoe sat parked on O'Donnell Street, he fast forwarded through the camera footage on his phone.

The Tahoe's interior was hot, as the AC was broken. No one knew when it had happened; this was just how the department had presented the vehicle to Silten and his team. No picking and choosing vehicles while on assignment; they worked with what they were given.

Inside the muggy cab sat four large ICE agents. The leader of the group, Silten, was a slicked-back all-business guy. With a full head of hair that extended to the back of his neck, he looked more like a rock star than an agent. His face was gaunt and angular, like a statue, and his eyes were sharp enough to slice through sheet metal. Prior to his time with ICE, he had served with the private military contractor Blackwater during the second Iraq War. To him, illegals were a pestilence in America that needed to be removed, cut out like cancer tumors if necessary.

The other three members of his team were McDonald, Tillman, and Peabody. A friend of Silten's, McDonald had been brought into the unit upon his recommendation. A competent agent and decently skilled with firearms and tech, McDonald felt right at home in ICE. He had a shaved head but kept a lengthy goatee to compliment his baldness. He had served alongside Silten in Blackwater years ago. Tillman was an ex-Marine, hot headed, and trigger happy. He looked it too, with his wiry hair and nimble frame, and was the kind of man who wanted any excuse to add extra holes to a person's body. During the war in Afghanistan, he had opened fire on unarmed civilians, causing the Marines to dishonorably discharge him. Due to the Marine Corps' insistence on covering up the incident, they never prosecuted him in any court. Last was Peabody. Compared to everyone else in the group, he was fucking useless. He had never served in any armed forces nor had any police, FBI, or DHS experience. In fact, he was a mechanic from South Carolina who had simply joined ICE due to the promise of a fifty thousand dollar starting bonus. The only thing Peabody was decent at was being a placeholder for a better agent whenever ICE decided he was too fat for service.

The second Tahoe sat parked behind Silten's. The voice of its driver, Jeffries, crackled to life on Silten's walkie-talkie. "Look, we got this bitch in the backseat. Why don't we just take her back while you guys hang here?"

Silten rolled his eyes and held up his walkie. "Because if we need to, we can use her as bait. When we get the kid, then we go back."

"All right, fine."

"Stop thinking so hard. You might hurt yourself."

Jeffries didn't reply.

"Fuck, I'm hungry," Peabody groaned.

"You're always hungry," Tillman exclaimed. "Maybe you can eat the kid when we catch him. How's that sound?"

"Fuck you, psycho."

"The fuck did you say to me?"

"Knock it off, you two," Silten screamed. "When we have them both, then you can butt fuck each other, like a couple of faggots, for all I care. Right now, just do what you're paid to do."

Silence fell over everyone in the Tahoe. After a beat, Peabody murmured to no one, "I still haven't even been paid at all."

"Got it!" McDonald raised his phone to Silten. "There's the license plate. Checking for LoJack now."

After another ten seconds, McDonald presented his phone to Silten again, which clearly displayed the Honda Accord's location—right around the corner in a derelict building.

***

"We're heading home now, Dad," Mateo said to the dashboard console, which Autumn had used to called Mateo's father.

"Good. When you get here, we'll figure this out," Marcus said. "Who's this person bringing you here?"

Autumn interjected, "Name's Autumn Frost. I'm a TAF driver."

"Okay, Ms. Frost. Keep my boy safe. I'll call the police. They'll be here when you arrive."

"Are you really sure you can trust them? They might take Mateo away too."

"We don't really have much choice. You can't fight them alone. I'm gonna call my lawyer too."

"One thing at a time. Make the call to the cops. We'll—"

"*You, in the building! Come out now or we go in guns blazing!*" The voice seemed to emanate from a loudspeaker outside the building.

"Fuck," Autumn yelled.

"What happened?" Marcus asked.

"Mr. Whatever-your-name-is, we'll call you back."

"My name is—"

Autumn pressed the End Call button on her console, grasped the key still inserted in the ignition, then started the engine.

"How did they find us?" Mateo asked, confused.

"Could have been anything. I don't know."

"*Last warning! Get out here*," the voice yelled again.

Autumn slowly pulled her seatbelt across her chest and buckled it, then desperately scanned for another exit. No other door was big enough to fit her vehicle, and ICE agents obviously guarded the busted doorway. No way out.

Except …

"Kid, do me a favor," Autumn ordered.

"Yeah?"

"Buckle up and keep your head down."

"What are you gonna do?"

"Something really fucking stupid. Hang on!"

Right as Mateo put his head between his legs, Autumn shifted into Drive, slammed on the gas pedal, and surged forward. She turned hard left and ascended the concrete ramp toward the one open door of the loading dock.

Chapter Three

The Accord breached the open loading bay. It burst forth like a rocket shooting off its launching pad. Engine roaring, the Accord went airborne for a split second, soared like a bird with wings made of bricks, then landed on the dusty concrete outside with a gut-wrenching *ka-thunk*! Autumn thought she heard something break under the hood but had no time to consider it. She gunned the engine and fishtailed onto the asphalt entry road, a trail of brown powdery dust spewing in her wake.

Behind the Accord, four ICE agents rounded the building and opened fire with single-shot bursts. *Pop pop pop pop*! Two rounds penetrated the Accord's trunk with metallic *plunk* sounds. One round blasted through the rear passenger window, spraying shattered glass all over Mateo. Terrified, he screamed and hunkered lower between his legs. To the right, on O'Donnell Street, Autumn saw the second Tahoe idling in wait for her to escape. Unfazed, Autumn kept going, hitting 50 mph as she turned left back onto O'Donnell Street. The second Tahoe darted forward and gave chase.

The road ahead was empty, not a car in sight. Autumn kept her foot on the gas. A rattling under the hood and a strange vibration in the gas pedal concerned her, yet she pressed on. Unlike movies and TV shows, where cars seemed impervious to damage, Autumn's Accord was already taking a beating from gunfire and gravity.

Behind the Accord, both Tahoes accelerated and continued their attack, like wild animals hunting their prey.

O'Donnell Street wrapped around the end of the overpass as it sloped to the ground, then leveled into a three-lane road. Autumn pushed the engine as hard as she could. A little luck rained upon her as she caught green lights the entire way. On the right stood more warehouses; on the left stretched a long row of low-income apartment buildings, more than likely Section 8 housing. That part of Baltimore contained the rundown areas where people only passed through on their routes to work. It was an endless series of gas stations, blank warehouses, and junk piles. Nothing good happened in that part of town, and Autumn's escape was only adding to that pedigree.

The Tahoes gunned their engines. Both vehicles lowered their front passenger windows, and the passengers aimed their firearms at the Accord five car lengths ahead. *Pop pop pop*! Shell cases ejected from the breaches and clattered along the passing road. Bullets zinged and whizzed harmlessly past the Accord. Oncoming fire during a chase was more hazardous to everything but the intended target. Wind resistance, gravity, and general shooter inaccuracy made driving while shooting more of a spray-and-pray method rather than a useful tactical option. It was all random chance if they could hit the Accord ahead of them.

Autumn kept her head low as she bobbed around a pair of slow-moving tractor trailers turning into a depot. The vibration in the pedal wasn't going away. Something was wrong with the car, and it would only get worse if they didn't stop to check the issue.

"Mateo, I need you up here," Autumn yelled.

"What?"

"I can't change my GPS and drive at the same time. I need you to navigate. Now, get up here!"

Mateo unbuckled his seatbelt and scrunched up as he crossed the center console and slid into the passenger seat. The force from Autumn weaving around another car shoved Mateo into the passenger door. He banged his face on the glass and yelped. He recovered and held his hand on his brow. A trickle of blood flowed down.

"Sorry. Buckle up, kid."

Mateo buckled again and sneered at Autumn. "Now what?"

The phone in the car rang. The listing read GOVERNMENT.

"Oh, this should be good," Autumn said, dripping with sarcasm. She pressed the Receive button on the console. "Twenty bucks says you're the assholes chasing us."

"You'd be right, Ms. Frost," Silten said. "Pull your fucking car over now and give us the kid. We might even let you go."

"Wow. You gotta learn how to lie better."

"You just don't fuckin' get it, do you? You're a fucking TAF driver. You're dead if you keep going."

"*Mmhmm.* Hey, you know how I like my whiskey?"

"How?"

"Neat. Because fuck ICE." She ended the call. "That felt good to say."

More shots rang out. One bullet hit the passenger side mirror and sheered it clean off. It fell and clattered to the road below, shattering into pieces. One of the chasing Tahoes ran over it and crushed it into even smaller bits.

"Shit! I need you to get me off this road," Autumn ordered. "We gotta get back into the city—somewhere we can ditch the car."

"Why?"

"Notice how they called me? They got my number, which means they have my LoJack too. They'll know where we are. We gotta get into a crowd, blend in. Plus, something is wrong with the car. It won't make it much farther, so find me the best, fastest route to the city."

Mateo snatched Autumn's phone from the dashboard console and entered the first address he could think of toward Baltimore—Camden Yards, home of the Baltimore Orioles. The GPS calibrated and a robotic woman's voice said, "Starting route to Camden Yards."

The route displayed on Autumn's dashboard console, then zoomed in on the next left turn to Dundalk Avenue, which led to Route 95—a four-way intersection and at an awkward angle. Four cars were stopped at the red light, waiting for it to change. The good luck from earlier had flipped back to Autumn's usual bad. She swerved right into the farthest lane. With no chance to take a left, and with no way could they stop without being shot, Autumn took a hard right onto Dundalk Avenue. It would buy her time to gain distance and to eventually pull a U-turn in the opposite direction.

She reeled around the right turn, barely missing an oncoming Dodge Charger, which swerved into the next lane while aggressively honking its horn. Autumn paid it no mind as she sped down the thin two-lane road, but traffic was light, allowing her to bob and weave around cars. She finally reached the next four-way intersection and nearly had a heart attack.

Another red light.

She stopped in the turn lane and craned around to look out the back window. The Tahoes were far away but would catch up soon. She faced forward to see the stop light remained red. She anxiously tapped her fingers on the wheel. *Come on, come on, come on!* She looked out the back again. The Tahoes were almost on them.

Mateo screamed, "It's green! *Go!*"

Autumn slammed on the gas pedal as she pulled a sharp U-turn. The car lurch hard as she turned. She and Mateo fought against the centrifugal force as the Tahoes caught up and made a desperate move. Both SUVs popped over the highway divider and crossed into the oncoming traffic.

"*Fuck!*" Autumn wrenched the steering wheel right. The Accord just barely merged into the right-hand lane, narrowly avoiding a collision with the beastly vehicles. It would take time for such large trucks to turn around, which would give them some distance. She kept her foot on the accelerator toward the Route 95 onramp.

Mateo, terrified, dry-heaved and leaned forward.

"Don't you dare puke in my car," Autumn yelled. She lowered the passenger window.

Mateo grasped the window edge and stuck out his head just as a stream of brown vomit sprayed from his mouth, splattering all over the passenger side of the car, leaving a kind of mud-colored trail. He heaved a second time and added to the first batch. When he finished, he slid inside and closed the window. "Sorry," he said, embarrassed.

"Just happy you did it out there."

Within ten seconds, the Accord ascended the onramp and entered traffic on Route 95 toward Baltimore. It was a busy day on the highway. People were either commuting home early for the weekend or heading into town to get parking for the parade. The white lines on the asphalt streaked by, moment by moment marking their distance. As they passed under a bridge, the city of Baltimore made itself present once again on the horizon. The downtown area was home to a pocket of tall buildings, though not quite skyscrapers. From the Accord's location, Autumn and Mateo could see Fells Point and, just beyond, Harbor East. Seeing the monolithic buildings in the distance,

Autumn had a feeling of security. They would be home free very soon.

Then she checked the GPS, and her eyes widened. "Wait, this goes to the tunnel."

"Yeah?"

"You're sending me to *the tunnel*?"

"You said the fastest route."

"I said the *best*, fastest route."

"This is the best route to get back to the city."

"What if the tunnel is blocked?!"

Mateo froze, realizing his error. "Oh."

"*Shit!*" Autumn did her best to veer into the right-hand lane, but traffic was too dense and blocked the path to the final turn-off before the Fort McHenry tunnel under the harbor. The tunnel connected the northern and southern sections of the Baltimore area, allowing commuters to reduce drive time and to avoid the inner city. It was high volume and almost always crowded. It was also a toll road, which meant Autumn would have to slow down for cameras as they exited the opposite side near Locust Point. On top of that, police cruisers heavily guarded it.

Out of options, Autumn eyed the distant Tahoes in the rearview mirror and gripped the steering wheel even harder. "Welp, guess we're goin' in."

The highway split into multiple pathways—over seven lanes—toward the distant toll booths. Each vehicle lethargically took their time, waiting for the toll camera to snap a photo of their license plate for future payment. Some vehicles had E-ZPass and skipped the line. Autumn had no E-ZPass, as she almost never traveled that far north and always avoided toll roads to save money. It was one of the things on her to-do list that she always seemed to forget. As they pulled up to the line, she told herself that if she survived this, she would get a pass ASAP.

The line moved agonizingly slow—so slow that if they didn't move within ten seconds, they'd be staring down the barrels of assault rifles.

With total disregard for everyone, Autumn said, "Fuck it." She bullied herself into the E-ZPass lane, narrowly avoiding collisions. She cut off vehicle after vehicle, received the customary honk, yell, and middle finger, then passed through the toll section. She would deal with the fallout of improper payment later.

Autumn looked back once again. The Tahoes were on her tail so close that one of the passengers stuck his head out the window and aimed to try his luck again. Autumn weaved, throwing off his aim as shots rang out. None connected. Traffic, noticing the chase, cleared away as the speeding vehicles passed. Just as the Accord and the Tahoes were about to enter the tunnel, a police cruiser on the shoulder noticed the chaos. The cruiser activated its lights and sirens and gave chase.

"Oh, come on," Autumn groaned.

The road sloped downward as the Accord entered the tunnel that was squared off with a long row of consecutive hot-white lighting fixtures in the corners of the roof that seemed to stretch forever. As the road sloped down, it curved slightly to the right, and a pair of solid white lines split the two lanes, implying a no-passing zone. There was barely enough room for normal traffic let alone any vehicle involved in a chase, and every car moved at the same 55 mph speed.

Autumn, careful to avoid innocent people, zipped around cars. Her steering wheel rumbled from whatever damage the axel had sustained. The Tahoes were close behind and gaining. Behind the Tahoes, a flurry of red and blue lights spun and illuminated the tunnel walls.

***

Inside the first Tahoe, Silten received a call from Jeffries: "Silten, we got blue on us."

"Handle it," Silten said, not breaking his hardened gaze from the road ahead.

"Handle it? How the fuck do we do that?"

"Get them off us. Be creative."

After a beat, Jeffries understood. "Got it." Jeffries turned around and nodded to one of the other agents in the car—a man named Caldwell. He lowered the rear driver's side window, stuck out his torso, and aimed his assault rifle. He flipped it to Full Auto and released a blaze of gunfire into the police cruiser's hood, shredding the engine.

Shell casings ejected from the breach and clattered to the blurry brown road below. Within a few seconds, plumes of black smoke and fire billowed from the edges of the cruiser's hood, blinding the driver. The cruiser slowed and eventually stopped in the middle of both lanes, blocking traffic.

Caldwell smirked beneath his black mask and slid inside. "It's done. Blue's gone."

In the back of the Jeffries's Tahoe, Juliana lay on the hard cargo-area floorboard, handcuffed and gagged. She mumbled something through her gag.

Caldwell leaned over the edge of the backseat and smacked her across the face. "Shut up, cunt!"

Jeffries called Silten again. "Silten, blue is all gone. Back in business."

"Good. We'll wait till we're out of the tunnel, then we get on both sides of her and box her in."

"Got it." Jeffries ended the call.

The Tahoes kept a steady pace, waiting for the next moment to strike. The Accord ahead of them was stuck behind a pair of vehicles that refused to speed up, and over the echo inside the tunnel came the sound of hollowed-out car horns at random intervals.

Silten quietly smiled to himself as he watched Frost struggle to escape. "That's right, bitch. You're goin' nowhere."

***

Honk honk honk. "Get outta the way!" Autumn smashed her hand into the steering wheel in frustration.

The Accord was stuck going the speed limit behind a panel van and beside a Mercedes to their left, which refused to accelerated despite Autmn's constant honking and yelling. Autumn saw the two trucks keeping a steady pace in her rearview mirror. They had stopped accelerating and weren't attempting to run them down any longer.

Confused, she said to Mateo, "They've stopped pressing on us. Kid, look back there and see what's going on."

Mateo turned and squinted out the back window. The second Tahoe moved into the left-hand lane and sped up to become parallel with the first Tahoe. "They're in both lanes now. They're not getting any faster, though."

Autumn glanced back to confirm. *What the fuck are you doing?* Autumn honked the horn again, but the two cars ahead ignored her. "Something's not right. Just keep watching, kid. We're almost out of the tunnel."

The brown-walled tunnel blurred by as they maintained speed. White light after white light zipped by overhead, until finally a brighter white light appeared ahead of them—the tunnel exit.

Autumn gripped the wheel hard at ten and two, waiting for the chance to get around the pair of assholes in front of her. She typically hated driving fast, preferring to get where she was going at a moderate pace. Today, though, would be an exception to that rule.

Meter by meter, the exit grew larger and brighter, until the flat-white light revealed the world above—Locust Point.

Once out of the tunnel, a third shoulder lane appeared on the far-left side of the road, divided from traffic by a solid yellow line. The Tahoes revved their engines and pulled ahead, one veering into the left shoulder lane, one tailgating the Accord. The left-lane Tahoe became parallel with the Accord. Autumn snapped her head left and saw the masked driver and passenger leering at her. It slowly dawned on her what was happening.

"Kid, duck again," Autumn ordered.

"What now?"

"They're trying to box us in. He's gonna take a swipe at us. Hang on!"

Autumn dashed into the middle lane and hit the brakes right as the Tahoe began its attack. The wheels screeched, and the steering wheel rumbled. Both vehicles just barely missed each other by centimeters. The Tahoe swerved across all three lanes, dove into the white concrete divider, and smashed the front right headlight. It regained control for a split second before the second Tahoe rear-ended it. Not enough to destroy the back of the vehicle but enough to force both trucks to stop.

Seeing her one opportunity, Autumn accelerated again and blazed passed the two crippled trucks. She glimpsed the driver of the rear vehicle screaming and yelling something. A flurry of gunshots filled the air and perforated the rear of the Accord. Autumn kept her head down and her foot on the gas pedal as they sped away.

Finally, out of the tunnel, Autumn swerved around the extra-slow van and Mercedes, gave them both the middle finger out the back window, and raced ahead of them. As she kept a tight grip on the wheel, she noticed how rough the car was riding. Something was really wrong under the hood.

"You can come up now, kid," Autumn said.

Mateo slowly raised his head from between his legs and looked around in amazement. They'd survived, somehow. "That was incredible."

"That was luck." She eyed the instrument panel and groaned. "And it looks like our luck just ran out. We gotta ditch this car fast."

"Why? What happened?"

"We're leaking fuel."

Chapter Four

The Accord died a split second after Autumn pulled into a lower-level parking spot in a garage on Howard Street. She shifted into Park, and it went kaput.

"Welp, that's the end of that," Autumn said. "Let's go. We gotta keep moving before they catch up."

Hurriedly, Autumn and Mateo exited the vehicle. The faint smell of gasoline filled the garage. Autumn circled the car and spotted three bullet holes right at the fuel tank. They were lucky to have made it back to the city.

"Shit," Autumn exclaimed. "You better be worth all this, kid."

"My dad has money. He can help."

"If we make it through this, I'll send him a bill."

Autumn opened the front-passenger door and retrieved some potentially useful items from the glove compartment—all nonlethal but still effective: mace, brass knuckles, an extendable baton, and a taser with three extra cartridges. After her adventure on New Year's Eve earlier that year, she figured it best to be prepared for any future mishaps. She snapped the bottle of mace onto her keychain, stuffed the brass knuckles and baton into her front pocket, and snapped a taser utility belt around her waist.

"What, are you trying to start a war?" Mateo asked.

"No, trying to stop one. Let's go." Autumn slammed the door and locked the car. On their way to the exit, Autumn called Becky.

After two rings, Becky answered. "Hey, babe, what's up? We're kinda backed up at the hospital right now. I can—"

"Becky, I'm kinda mixed up in something. I'm stuck in Baltimore, and the car's dead."

"Oh shit. What happened now?"

"Pissed off the wrong people. Got this kid I'm trying to watch after, but whoever is after him got his mom already."

Autumn and Mateo entered the bright sunlight on Howard Street.

"Jesus Christ, is it gang members?"

"*Uh*, yeah. Kinda. It's ICE."

"Are you fucking serious?"

"We lost them already, but they might be tracking us. Gonna have to ditch our phones so they can't find where we are. We'll hide out somewhere."

"No, keep your phones. You'll need them in an emergency. Do you have anything metal that you could wrap your phone in? Foil or something?"

"Why the fuck would I carry tinfoil with me? What kinda…" Autumn remembered the meal she had bought for Becky at Ellie's Tavern. The fried calamari were wrapped in foil to keep it warm on the drive home. "Actually, yeah. I think I might have something."

"Good. Wrap your phone and stay out of sight. I have a friend in the Baltimore Police who could help you guys out."

"Cops help ICE, Becky. That's no good."

"Trust me, he hates them as much as we do. His name is Trevor. You'll be safe once he finds you. I'll call him directly so this doesn't get dispatched over the police band. Unwrap your phone in twenty minutes so he can text you. Is there anywhere you can hide?"

Autumn observed her surroundings. She had been to Baltimore many times, though mainly with friends for Orioles baseball games. This section of town was relatively familiar. The Inner Harbor was to the south, the CFG Events Arena was to the north, and east and west were a long stretch of road that connected the business districts. Everywhere she looked in her immediate vicinity, though, were the same things: Starbucks, 7-Eleven, CVS, occasional department stores, chain restaurants—everything a capitalist hellscape required. No place in the area was suitable for hiding out. Cameras were everywhere. If ICE could track Autumn through her LoJack, they could definitely find her through facial recognition.

She looked south on Howard Street at a crowd walking along Pratt Street, the main artery for traffic next to the Inner Harbor. And on that day, the Baltimore Pride Parade occupied it, marching along in a rhythm to pop music.

"I think we have a place to go. We'll be on Pratt Street. Gotta go now. Love ya, babe."

"Love you too. Please don't do anything stupid."

"Me? No way." As Autumn ended the call, she rushed back into the garage.

Mateo trailed after her, asking what she was doing. She ignored him and popped open the rear door to retrieve the bag of calamari. Just as she remembered, tinfoil wrapped the meal. She dumped the calamari out of the foil and put it directly into the Styrofoam tray. She tore the eighteen-by-eighteen-inch foil down the middle, handed half to Mateo, and pulled out her phone.

"Wrap your phone up. Now!"

Mateo obeyed. "What's this supposed to do?"

"In case they're tracking our phones, that will stop the signal for getting out. Help is on the way. Let's head to Pratt Street."

"What's on Pratt Street?"

Autumn shot Mateo a smile. "I wanna watch the parade."

***

"What do you mean, *they're gone*?" Silten yelled.

"Just that. They were there; now they're not," McDonald informed. "Still got a read on the car, though."

"Fine, we'll start there. Where are they?"

McDonald zeroed in on the Accord's location. The digital map showed a green box with a red blinking dot in the middle. "Parking garage on South Howard Street."

Silten radioed Jeffries. "Parking garage on South Howard Street. Is the bitch giving you any trouble?"

"No, she's quiet now," Jeffries said.

"Good. Let's finish this."

The pair of Tahoes exited I-95 North toward Baltimore. They followed the 395 offramp onto Cal Ripken Way, which passed by Camden Yards.

As Silten's Tahoe drove down the road, McDonald said, "My dad used to take me to every O's game."

"The O's are fucking shit," Silten fired back.

McDonald shrugged in agreement. "Yeah, I know. But… home team, ya know?"

Traffic backed up as the agents approached Conway Street. A homeless veteran wandered between the cars in traffic, begging for change. With nowhere to go, Silten and McDonald stared straight ahead, pretending to not notice the man. At the last second, McDonald flitted his gaze toward the homeless man.

Seeing a spark of interest, the vet knocked on the passenger-side window. "Hey, you guys got any change? A dolla'?"

Silten and McDonald sat still, said nothing.

"I know you see me. And I see you. I just need a little change."

Annoyed, Silten lowered the passenger window. The smell of dirty clothes and alcohol wafted into the truck. "You want some change?" Silten drew his sidearm and aimed at the veteran's head. "I'll change your fucking life if you don't step away from the vehicle!"

The vet recoiled. "What the fuck? I just needed help. You ICE fucks are all the same. I bled for this country!" Distraught, the vet wandered farther down the line of cars.

As the vet trudged off, Silten yelled after him, "And you'll bleed for it again if you ever come back!" Silten holstered his sidearm and chuckled at McDonald. "Man, I miss our Blackwater days."

McDonald smirked through his mask.

Traffic trudged along, held up by the pride parade ahead of them. They eventually reached South Howard Street after a series of twists and turns to circumnavigate the parade route. It was an annoyance, but they found the garage where the Accord was parked. The Tahoes illegally parked outside the entrance to the garage, blocking a small green Toyota from exiting. As the driver stepped out to complain, the two squads of agents aimed rifles at the driver. Terrified, the driver retreated into their car. Jeffries stayed behind in his truck to watch their captive.

They moved like a mob of thugs through the garage, weapons drawn. The garage was packed on account of the parade down the street. Once they spotted the Accord, they raised their rifles, flipped off their safeties, and trained their sights on the driver's seat.

"Outta the car! Right now," Silten ordered.

No movement. The distant sound of pop music echoed through the garage. Peabody recognized the music—Taylor Swift—though he kept that information to himself.

Silten eyed Tillman, then tilted his head toward the car. Tillman stepped forward, more than happy to take point. With his gun at the ready, he circled around the car and approached the driver's side door. He looked inside and saw no one. Furious, he smashed the driver's side window with the butt of his gun, which triggered the car alarm. He reached inside, unlocked the door, snapped it open, and found the hood latch. With a soft *pop*, the hood rose half an inch. Tillman opened the hood, reached for the battery, and ripped out the connection cables. The alarm died.

Tillman slammed down the hood, disappointed. "Nothing, boss. They're gone."

"Fuck," Silten growled. He sat in the driver's seat of the Accord and inspected everything. Center console, glove compartment, under the seats, and the backseat floorboard. Aside from the car registration and owner's manual, all he found was a Styrofoam box of lukewarm calamari. He exited the car, holding the box.

As Silten shut the door, Peabody asked, "What's that?"

"Fried calamari. Want some, fat ass?" As he walked past, Silten chucked the box in Peabody's face. It fell and broke open upon the gasoline-stained concrete.

Silten walked out onto South Howard Street to look around. Frost and the kid could be anywhere by that point. How they had lost signal on their cellphones was a mystery. The timeframe of losing their cell signals and locating the vehicle in the garage was only around twenty minutes. They could be far but not that far. If the cell service was offline, that meant they weren't using them at all. No cabs, no railway, no bus. They were on foot. But where, was the question.

The music down street annoyed Silten. He stared at the parade on Pratt Street, furious. Then he had an epiphany.

McDonald walked alongside Silten. "What now, boss? Just settle for the woman and call it quits?"

"No. If you were being tracked, where do you think it would be best to hide?" Silten pointed down the street.

McDonald nodded at the distant parade. "In a crowd, in plain sight."

"That's right. Load up. We're moving out."

***

Colored flags billowed in the wind. Rainbows littered the street. People of all types—White, Black, Asian, Indian, disabled, bisexual, trans—marched as one in celebration of their unity as a people. Loud joyful pop music echoed off the buildings and filled the warm harbor air. Several trucks with parade signs slowly traversed Pratt Street, keeping pace with the crowd. On the sidewalks, crowds watched and waved, expressing their support for the LGBT community. Also among the crowd was a congregation of protesters spouting religious hate, condemning the entire parade as a demonic act.

Among all this, Autumn and Mateo kept a low profile and hid among the sidewalk onlookers.

Over the loud music, Mateo yelled, "So, when is this friend of yours supposed to show up?"

"I'm gonna check my phone in a few minutes. You think your dad can straighten this out for us?"

"He should. He's got money, and he's up there in the government."

"Wait, what?"

"Yeah, he works in Baltimore for the government. Not really sure what he does, though."

"Well, that's comforting."

A pair of large-breasted women passed on the street and waved at Autumn. One blew her a kiss.

"Goddamn. I wish Becky could see this."

"Who's Becky anyway?"

"Girlfriend. She works at Anne Arundel Medical Center. I was about to take her something to cat till you interrupted my day."

"I'm sorry. I didn't know what else to do."

"It's fine. Not like you're the first."

"What do you mean? You've done this before?"

"Every so often. Long story." Autumn scanned the crowd. No sign of the ICE agents. "All right, I'm gonna check my phone." She pulled her foil-wrapped phone from her pocket and unwrapped it. Within a few seconds, signal had returned, though it was spotty due to the high crowd density. Paranoid, she looked around again. Still nothing. As she looked down, a text message popped up.

TREVOR: *Autumn, this is Trevor Brand. Becky told me what's happening. I'm almost to Pratt Street. It's my day off, so I'll be in regular clothes. Here's a photo of me.*

The photo took an obscene amount of time to load, but it finally loaded. Trevor Brand was a Black man, with short-cropped hair, mid-30s, clean shaven, light-colored eyes, chiseled jaw. Were Autumn more interested in men than women, she would've considered giving him a shot. Not a bad looking guy at all.

Autumn screenshotted the chat.

AUTUMN: *Got it. Me and the kid are hiding in the crowd. Here's a photo of where we are. Putting my phone away once this goes through.*

Autumn snapped a pic of the street straight ahead of her. In the background was the Baltimore Convention Center, an obvious and impossible-to-miss landmark. Autumn waited for the photo to send, then closed her phone, rewrapped it, and shoved it into her pocket.

All they could do was wait.

***

"Hang on," McDonald yelled. "I had her for a sec."

"Where?" Silten asked.

"Just like you thought. Pratt Street. They're in the crowd."

The Tahoes beamed down the road toward Pratt Street. As they approached, they decelerated and illegally parked in a bus lane. All the agents disembarked and huddled up.

"All right, Jeffries and Peabody, stay here and watch the trucks. Everyone else on me."

"Why do I have to stay here instead of one of Jeffries's guys?" Peabody asked.

"Because it's a tightly packed crowd that doesn't allow too much beef with broccoli, you fat fuck. Stay here and shut up."

Silten and the other five agents—McDonald, Tillman, Caldwell, Arnold, and Winslow—unassumingly shoulder-sliced through the crowd to search for their prey, until random panicked shouts erupted. "ICE is here!" "Everybody run! It's ICE!" "Run before they grab you!" Silten and the crew shoved people out of the way and tripped others who attempted to escape, inciting a small patch of chaos.

The parade continued, though some performers noticed the brutality occurring to the side and dialed 9-1-1.

***

"Oh shit," Autumn yelled. Thirty feet away, Autumn saw the agents. She ducked and pulled Mateo down with her. "All right, stick with me, kid. We gotta move."

She crouch-walked through the crowd, gently pushing people aside, as she tightly held Mateo's hand. Through the noise and sea of bodies, Autumn searched desperately for some kind of exit. Multiple times, she bumped into someone, leading to said person gazing down in confusion. "Sorry, sorry," Autumn said.

As they passed Pratt Street Ale House, Autumn bumped into a large Black man wearing jeans and a brown T-shirt. By sheer luck, she had found Trevor Brand.

Autumn stood. Mateo did the same.

"Guessing you're Autumn. Becky—"

"Later. We have—"

Over the noise of the crowd, an agent screamed, *"Silten! There! I found 'em!"*

Autumn slumped as groaned, "Will this day never end?"

Chapter Five

Chaos erupted as the agents shoved people out of the way. The music continued, though no one was dancing; the parade had come to a complete stop. People ran in every direction to seek escape. It was an awkward moment to see armed masked men marching down the sidewalk, looking for trouble, while Taylor Swift sang on and on about trouble. For Autumn, Mateo, and Trevor, it was terrifying.

Trevor stepped forward and extended one hand while grasping for his off-duty sidearm. "Lower your weapons. These two are—"

"*Gun,*" Tillman yelled.

The agents aimed their rifles at the three individuals, though the crowd obstructed their line of sight.

Trevor released his hand from his sidearm and held out both arms, pleading. "No, I'm a cop! Baltimore Police!"

Tillman struggled to get through the crowd as people repeatedly shoved him. Finally, in sheer anger and hatred for the environment, he aimed his rifle skyward and let off three rounds. *Bang! Bang! Bang!*

The crowd dropped low to the ground. Screams everywhere. ICE was in the house. The crowd, just as quickly as they had dropped, got up and bolted in all directions.

Trevor drew his sidearm. "Everyone, stay on the ground! Stay down!"

Seeing her one chance, Autumn grabbed Mateo's hand and dragged him away. They sprinted around the corner of Pratt Street Ale House and headed up Hopkins Place. They passed a Days Inn to their left as they bounded up the incline. Behind them, several shots rang out. Autumn couldn't tell who was shooting, Trevor or the ICE agents. "Come on, kid. Move!"

"I *am* moving!" The incline up Hopkins Place was rough—an uneven sidewalk and traffic going in and out of the hotel. It was enough to rapidly drain anyone.

"Wait," boomed a voice behind them. Trevor rounded the corner and followed them. Part of his shirt was bloody. As a Baltimore Police officer, he was in solid physical shape and caught up quickly. Noticing Mateo's lethargy, he shoved the boy by the waist and matched Autumn's pace. "My car is up there in the garage!"

"Good. And I'm driving," Autumn dictated.

"My car?"

"Yeah. You're bleeding."

Trevor glimpsed his bloody shirt. He slowed his sprint and patted his chest, searching for a bullet hole. He found it in his left shoulder. It was clean through and bleeding badly.

"How the fuck didn't you notice that?" Autumn asked.

"Adrenaline. Cuts off pain receptors. I'll feel it when I come down." Trevor turned toward Pratt Street to see the agents maneuver through the panicking crowd and round the corner. Trevor heard Silten yell, "There they are! Come on, boys! Get their asses!"

The trio darted as fast as possible. When they reached the top of the incline on Hopkins Place, Trevor pointed across the street to an underground garage. Ignoring passing traffic, they crossed the street and entered the dark descending tunnel.

"Okay, now I feel it," Trevor admitted. He clutched his wound to stop the bleeding.

"Then gimme your keys while you can still move your arm," Autumn demanded.

Wincing in pain, Trevor retrieved his car keys from his left pocket.

Autumn snatched them and noticed the brand label. "Subaru? You drive a *Subaru*?"

"Yeah?"

"I didn't know you were gay too."

"That's hilarious. Becky said you had a smart mouth."

"Heh, she would know best."

The garage was a typical drab underground garage—beige concrete everywhere, sterile artificial lighting every few meters, oil stains in every parking spot, and a slight slant to the floor. On the way in, Autumn noticed the candy-cane-colored boom arm and ticket booth. How they would get past that without ICE catching them was a problem for five-minutes-in-the-future Autumn. Trevor had parked on P2, which meant taking the stairs down to the next level.

The trio descended. As they entered P2, a weird smell of rotting trash emanated from some unknown location. Autumn stifled a gag as she rounded a corner and saw the culprit—an overflowing trashcan topped with a pile of vomit. *This fucking town, I swear.*

"My car is down the next row," Trevor said. "Follow me."

"Hey, thanks for doing this. I'm sorry you got shot," Autumn said.

"Actually, with this wound, this could help build a case against ICE. Firing at an off-duty cop? Yeah, that would definitely hit them hard."

"They've gotten away with everything else they've ever done. You think they care?"

After a moment's consideration, Trevor realized Autumn was right. ICE operated with almost total impunity. Murders, assaults, and kidnappings were just another day with them. Why would shooting an off-duty officer add up to anything? Especially a *Black* police officer in Baltimore. Trevor shook his head and accepted the defeat.

With disappointment coating his voice, Trevor said, "Car is right there." He pointed to a blue Subaru Impreza.

Autumn hit the Unlock button twice. *Beep beep!* She slid into the driver's seat and buckled up. Trevor slowly rolled into the front passenger seat, groaning at the pain returning to his body from his diminishing adrenaline high. Mateo hopped into the backseat and buckled up.

"Kid, you illegal?" Trevor asked.

"No, I live in Canton."

"Then why the fuck—"

Autumn shot a hard glare at Trevor, as if telepathically saying, *Really? You still don't get it?*

Trevor shrugged and buckled his seatbelt.

Autumn spotted the manual gear shift and noticed the well-worn steering wheel. More than likely, Trevor had purchased the car used. Something cheap and efficient to get around and to fit into a police officer's budget. Nothing fancy, like Autumn's Honda Accord. Plain Jane normal.

With ease, Autumn slid the key into the ignition, turned it, and the car purred to life. The car rumbled, and the engine sounded louder than a normal Subaru. "Did you put a supercharger in this thing?"

"Yeah," Trevor said, clasping his shoulder. "Figured it was best to have it in case of an emergency."

"Oh, I could kiss you right now."

"Just get us outta here first. Besides, I'm married." Trevor held up his left hand and gently rubbed the bottom of a wedding band.

"Man or woman?" Autumn asked.

"Woman."

"Damn. You could have totally justified why you had a Subaru."

"Oh, shut up, Frost."

"*Umm*, what's a supercharger?" Mateo asked.

"You're about to find out, kid." Autumn smirked, shifted into Reverse, pulled out of the parking spot, and quickly shifted into First. The Subaru screeched and surged forward across the concrete floor.

Driving a manual was much different from driving an automatic. It required precise timing and full attentiveness. Miss an upshift and the engine belt could miss the next gear and cause the engine to overrev. Miss a downshift and the car could jerk forward and cause the engine to stall out. It was like a rhythm game. While Autumn had driven her fair share of manuals, she had grown accustomed to the ease of automatics. That said, manuals still had their share of superior features, such as better control of speed and acceleration, as well as better fuel economy. In a chase, all those features were critical.

As the car ascended the ramp, she checked the fuel gauge—just over half a tank. More than enough to put some distance between them and ICE.

The floor leveled out again and was a straight shot for the exit. The garage entrance burned white hot and misty from light distortion. The hazy light wrapped around Autumn's next obstacle—the ticket booth. No way could they stop and pay the toll. Only one solution.

Adding more pressure to the accelerator, Autumn said, "Trevor …"

"Just do it! If you get a ticket, I'll tear it up."

Autumn shifted into Second. A fury of fuel pumped into the engine. It roared like a wild animal. "Kid, duck!"

The trio ducked in unison. The car ascended the short ramp, bounced once, and punched through the boom arm, leaving a long horizontal gash across the hood. As the Subaru returned to the world above, ICE agents rushed toward the garage entrance from the left. Autumn locked gazes with one of the agents, probably the leader, and scowled at him. She turned hard right and raced away, shifting into Third as she sped toward Uptown.

Automatic gunfire rang out. *Ratatatatat!* Multiple rounds hit the trunk and blew out the rear window. The howling wind rushed in as shards of glass showered upon Mateo. While driving up Hopkins Place, Autumn realized it was a one-way street. With the slightest shred of luck, no traffic was headed her way, which gave her the chance to pass through the intersection and onto Park Avenue, which flowed in the proper direction.

As Autumn weaved around traffic, she glanced in the rearview mirror at the two accelerating Tahoes homing in on the Subaru's tail.

"Fuck, this hurts," Trevor groaned.

Autumn eyed the damage to Trevor's shoulder. It was bloody, pulpy, and worsening by the second. "You got a first aid kit in here?"

"Yeah, in the trunk." Blood from Trevor's hand dripped onto the seat.

"Oh, we ain't stopping. Kid, check the backseat. See if you can open it from in here."

Mateo unbuckled his belt to look for a handle. The Subaru hit a deep pothole and bounced hard. Mateo's right hand landed in pile of sharp glass, giving him a half dozen small cuts.

"Fuck," Autumn yelled. "Sorry. I hate the roads here."

"Everybody does," Trevor murmured.

Pushing through the pain, Mateo found a circular strap in the center of the backseat. He backed up to gain leverage, pulled, and the seat flipped down, revealing the darker interior of the trunk space. "Where is it?"

"Right side. Against the wall," Trevor said.

Mateo felt around in the void. Eventually, he found it, ripped it off the Velcro straps on the wall, and turned around. He thrust his arm between the two front seats to present it to Autumn like a gift.

"What the fuck do you want me to do with that?" Autumn exclaimed. "I'm driving."

"You're gonna have to help me, kid," Trevor said.

"Oh shit. Okay, what do you need?"

"Gauze. All of it."

Autumn downshifted to Second as they approached a red light. She realized the one miscalculation with having a manual during a chase was how it was only efficient when not needing to stop for traffic lights every other block.

The Subaru slowed as it bounded around traffic to gain even the slightest bit of extra distance from the Tahoes. Heading away from the Inner Harbor meant less traffic, but it also meant a rougher ride.

Park Avenue was a wretched road. Street lines were barely visible, and parked cars packed both sides. One of the biggest design issues with Baltimore's inner city was the width of streets. Like Annapolis, Baltimore was a colonial town, and the city could only widen its streets so much before massive changes to infrastructure needed to occur. Annapolis, however, had managed to adapt to this issue and maintained it streets properly. Baltimore, however, had fallen into disarray and never seemed to improve. Streets were always patchy, pockmarked, or even downright undrivable. Factor in a car with manual shifting, and it was a recipe for grinding gears.

Autumn maintained a moderate pace ascending Park Avenue. It was a slight incline heading Uptown. She glanced left and right at the passing buildings. Graffiti everywhere, shuttered businesses, trash piled in gutters. Outside of small pockets of beauty, Baltimore was a sad, broken town.

Trevor reached back and grabbed a packet of gauze from Mateo. He ripped open the package and shoved the entire white square patch into the bullet hole. He winced and stifled a yell as he tightly packed it. A small tuft still emanated from the hole, but the front was patched up. "Okay, kid. Your turn."

"*What?*"

"I can't reach my shoulder. You have to do it."

"Are you serious?"

"Kid, either do it," Autumn interjected, "or I'll dump you on the sidewalk and just take him to the hospital alone. Your choice."

Mateo sighed heavily, then bounced again as Autumn hit massive bump in the road.

"Sorry again," Autumn said. "Do the thing already!"

Mateo pulled out another packet of gauze, ripped it open, then hovered over Trevor's left shoulder.

Trevor leaned forward. "Just pack it all the way in. It'll stop the bleeding."

"God, I'm gonna puke." Mateo rounded the gauze pad and pressed it into the bullet wound. It slid in, got stuck for a moment, but eventually found its home inside Trevor's shoulder. The white gauze slowly reddened. The tip of Mateo's finger found its way half an inch into the hole as he packed in the last bit of gauze. Unable to stop himself, Mateo lowered the driver's side window, leaned out, and vomited.

"Kid, how much is still inside you?" Autumn asked.

From behind the Subaru, distant pops rang out. Gunshots.

Mateo fell limp and hung halfway out the window.

"Kid," Trevor yelled.

"What's wrong?" Autumn shifted into Third as she saw all the green traffic lights ahead. At least half a mile of clear open road lay before them.

Trevor fought through the pain, turned around, and pulled Mateo inside. Mateo's body fell limp on the backseat, blood streaking his head.

Autumn looked in her rearview mirror and gasped. "Oh my God, is he dead?"

Trevor felt a pulse on Mateo's neck, still steady. He checked the wound on his head. A small red slash ran across the scalp but no damage to the skull. "He's okay. It just barely grazed him. Impact must've knocked him out. He's super lucky."

"Can't keep leaning on luck. We need to get outta here somehow. Is there any place we can go that gets them off our tail?"

Trevor touched his dashboard console. A built-in GPS screen showed their exact location. He pressed a few buttons and scanned for public locations. "Mount Vernon. Head toward the Washington Monument. There's a roundabout we can use to get them off us and buy time."

Autumn obliged. She continued along Park Avenue till she reached an intersection for West Monument Street. She turned right, following the onboard GPS, and in the distance saw what Trevor was referring to. The Baltimore Washington Monument was nothing like the one in Washington, DC beyond the obvious phallic design. It was rounded instead of squared, and the top looked like a lookout tower, with a statue of George Washington standing on its peak. In many ways, it much more closely resembled a giant penis than the one in DC. At the base was a squared-off building for entrance to the phallic structure designed for tours.

West Monument Street ended at the roundabout and split like a T-section heading to Cathedral Street. Autumn ignored all the traffic, zipped right, then immediately left again to get onto West Mount Vernon Place. This double lane road lead directly to the cobblestone roundabout.

Autumn's hand was exhausted and cramped from constantly shifting up and down, up and down. She was tired, and when she entered the roundabout, she missed a gear and heard the engine grind; a shrill *rrrreeeee* erupted from the engine for a moment, then faded away.

As she began to circle the roundabout, the tires let out a staccato *thud thud thud thud* over the cobblestones. Asphalt covered the surrounding streets, but the city had maintained that one section for historical purposes.

"Okay. Now what?" Autumn asked. As she circled, she honked her horn, forcing people to stay out of the traffic.

"Once they get on the cobblestone, go east down the hill toward St. Paul. There's a three-way split on that road."

Autumn scanned for the Tahoes. Finally, they appeared and entered the roundabout from the opposite side of the Subaru's position. The Subaru and the Tahoes were like opposite blades of a fan spinning around its hub, locked in a left-turning unison. Suddenly, the rear Tahoe stopped dead in its tracks, waiting for Autumn to pass once again.

"Shit! Now or never, Frost."

Autumn took her first chance and exited the roundabout onto East Mount Vernon Place. Unfortunately, it was the wrong side. She headed directly into incoming traffic. Another car sped toward her. Without thinking, she cut hard right, mounted the curb, barreled through a pair of bushes, and landed in the grassy divider between the two lanes. It was a wide space but filled with trees, bushes, benches, and people. She downshifted again, missed a gear, heard the grinding, then felt a moment of relief when the engine finally caught back up. She slammed on the horn, and people ran for cover.

"What the fuck, Frost?"

"Stop with the goddamn yelling. I'm making this up as I go."

"I can fucking see that!"

Autumn saw the Tahoes following in her rearview mirror—one mounted the grassy divider; one stayed in the outgoing traffic lane. Out of options, she took the last chance she had. She cut hard left, squeezed the Subaru between two trees, bounced off the sidewalk, and reentered the incoming traffic lane. One Tahoe attempted to follow, crashed, and became wedged between both trees, too wide for the gap.

Weaving around incoming traffic, Autumn said, "That's one down. One to go."

They finally reached St. Paul Street. Autumn turned right off East Mount Vernon and surged forward, upshifting into Second. The second Tahoe fell in behind the Subaru, nearly clipping their bumper, but with a supercharger under the Subaru's hood, Autumn had the better gear for acceleration.

Half a mile down the road, St. Paul split into a Y-section—one road heading upward, one staying flat and heading toward a short tunnel. More shots rang out. None connected.

"I'm really fucking sick of these guys," Autumn shouted.

"You and everyone else," Trevor blurted back.

Autumn stayed to the left, preferring the tunnel. The Tahoe was now three car lengths behind them. If they could gain enough distance, traffic lights could impede them.

As they crossed the intersection and headed toward the tunnel, Autumn saw a small pedestrian walkway, just big enough for a compact car, on the right that led to the upper section of the Y-route. She seized the opportunity, wrenched the wheel right, and mounted the small curb to gain access to the concrete walkway. It was a tight squeeze but just enough to make it to the second road. The Tahoe would be trapped on the road toward the tunnel.

Autumn maneuvered the Subaru up the walkway, honking at pedestrians to get out of the way. She grazed a tire on the right side and missed a gear, but eventually she made it, dismounted the curb, and entered the roadway.

With ICE long gone and without a way to track them, Autumn finally relaxed. Her hands shook, and a river of sweat ran down her back, soaking through her green tank top.

"Jesus Christ, Frost. I don't know how the fuck you pulled that off," Trevor said.

"Must've been divine intervention, I guess."

The pair of them laughed as the Subaru settled into a cruising speed down St. Paul. She took the first right turn to gain distance in case ICE circled around to retrace the Subaru's path. She put three solid blocks between them and St. Paul, spotted a parking garage, and went up to the top deck, four stories high.

As Autumn pulled into a parking space, Mateo groaned and awoke from his slumber. "Oh, what happened?"

"You missed all the fun, kid," Trevor jested. "She just saved your ass. Again."

Chapter Six

The sun was setting across Baltimore. Golden rays of light sliced through the gaps between buildings and fell across a sea of car windshields backed up in traffic. It was just after 6 p.m., and everyone was calling it quits, fighting for lane space to leave town. Small packs of pedestrians jaywalked to parking garages and crossed crosswalks at inappropriate times to gain those precious extra ten seconds, hoping to get at least one more car length ahead in the gridlock. Despite the traffic, at the right time of day, with the right kind of light, the Inner Harbor could be dazzlingly beautiful.

Four blocks away, on the top deck of a parking garage, Trevor Brand lay under his car in an oil slick, attempting to patch a hole in his oil pan with sealant. Autumn's hardcore driving didn't come without an asterisk.

Meanwhile, Autumn was ripping apart the Subaru's interior looking for the vehicle's LoJack. If ICE could find her Accord, they could find Trevor's Subaru. She checked under the dashboard—nothing. Inside the glove compartment—nada. The center console—nope. She popped the hood, checked the car battery, and found it zip tied to the car frame. "Hey, you got any snips?"

"Any what?" Trevor asked through an opening in the engine. Autumn's face was just visible through a small gap.

Autumn craned her head downward for a better view of Trevor. "Snips. Like, cutters. Or a knife."

"Yeah, check the trunk. Tools are in there."

As Autumn walked to the trunk, she peeked through the rear window at a shellshocked Mateo sitting in the center seat, silently staring straight ahead. She couldn't help but feel sorry for him. He'd done nothing to deserve the day he'd had. She held onto that thought as she opened the trunk to reveal a wide array of tools—tire iron, car jack, spare tire under a mat, socket wrenches, spare quarts of oil, road flares bundled on the wall, and many other random things. A set of dirty clothes was also shoved into the back corner. She dug around and finally found a pair of wire cutters.

Autumn headed to the engine, reached in, and snipped the zip ties. The LoJack fell away immediately, dangled for a second by its red connector wire, then Autumn dragged it up and ripped it out. She walked to the edge of the rooftop, heaved back, and chucked it as far as she could. "Hope it lands on a Republicans windshield."

Trevor laughed under the car.

Autumn opened the rear door and kneeled. "Hey, you okay, kid?"

Mateo said nothing.

"Yeah, I know what you mean." Autumn slid into the backseat and shut the door. "*Hmph.* It's comfy in here."

Mateo said nothing.

Autumn wrapped her arm around his shoulder. "Look, kid, we're gonna find your mom and get you home. You'll be all right."

Finally, he cracked and cried into Autumn's chest. She held him as he wailed and screamed.

Trevor, hearing the noise, came up from the ground, hands soaked in oil and sealant. He gazed inside.

Autumn held Mateo and rocked him. When she noticed Trevor looking inside, she shrugged at him and held the kid tightly. Minutes passed before the scared kid finally got it all out.

Autumn released her hold on him. "We'll figure this out, Mateo. You'll be fine. Okay?"

"Okay," Mateo responded weakly. "Thank you, Autumn."

"You're welcome. Now let's get your head fixed." Autumn reached for the med kit. She looked inside for anything she could use as a bandage. Mateo's wound was in an odd place, so all she could use was a gauze roller bandage. First, she sterilized the wound with alcohol pads, then she unraveled a two-foot-long length and wrapped the circumference of Mateo's head. When she had expended the entire roll, she used a clip to secure the end.

Mateo looked more like he'd had a root canal than a head injury, but the bandage would work for the moment. "If I had more, I'd turn you into a mummy."

Mateo chuckled.

Trevor tapped on the passenger window.

"Be right back," Autumn said. Autumn slid out and closed the rear door.

"Take a walk with me," Trevor said.

Autumn walked around the car and joined Trevor near the roof's edge, twenty feet from the car.

"We are in some deep shit, Autumn," Trevor stated.

"Oh, really? What was your first clue?" Autumn leaned forward and rested her forearms on the concrete wall surrounding the roof. The sun slowly dipped behind a building and cast a pillar of darkness in a diagonal direction across several streets below.

"I'm serious, Frost. These guys are fucking cowboys. They don't give a shit who gets hurt. What the hell did this kid do?"

"No idea. He said *nothing*." Autumn watched Mateo wrap his hand in a gauze pad to cover the glass cuts. "I believe him, though. You know how ICE operates. They go after anyone, regardless of info. They have his mother, too. Picked her up earlier today. He ran, ended up in my car, and a bunch of winding roads later, here we are."

"Fuck." Trevor joined Autumn on the concrete wall, resting his arms and watching the traffic below. "Yeah. Fuck."

"I think it might be time to call in some back up."

"Like whom? The rest of the cops?"

"Yeah. The rest of the cops."

"Look. I appreciate everything you've done for us today, and Becky recommended you because you feel the same way about those chucklefucks as I do, but you know what they're gonna do if we get the Baltimore Police involved. They're gonna turn him over to them. You know it."

Trevor, a solid foot taller than Autumn, glanced over her head at Mateo. "Not necessarily."

"Something I don't know?"

"You remember when we were on Pratt Street? When they fired into the crowd during the parade?"

Like a bolt of lightning, it finally struck Autumn how they could get out of their predicament. "Cameras everywhere. Putting us at the scene, running away, and they're firing into an innocent crowd. Baltimore Police would have to hold the kid for questioning, because it would be part of an active investigation."

"Exactly. At least the kid would be safe for a while, and you'd be off the hook for a lot; though, I don't really know what you were doing before I showed up."

"I'm sure I have some traffic violations headed my way in the mail."

"Better than a bullet in the head, Frosty."

"*Frosty*?"

"Yeah, that's your name now. When you were driving, you kept it cool, didn't flip out. Military guys like to say some shit like *stay frosty*, or something like that."

Autumn chuckled at her new nickname. "You're so lucky I like you. I typically hate cops."

"Do I give off the smell of bacon that badly?"

"*Eh*, not really. I would have pinned you more for a firefighter or something."

"Maybe in another life."

"The kid mentioned his dad works in the local government too. Maybe we can use that to our advantage."

"Wouldn't hurt. Did he mention what he actually does, though? Janitor at city hall is a little different from a councilman."

"He didn't say. We got interrupted during our last conversation. But we can still ask him. Might be worth something."

The pair went silent and watched the sun dip below the last building before disappearing over the horizon.

"All right," Trevor said, "I'm gonna make the call."

"Good luck." Autumn peered over her shoulder a Mateo, who had finished wrapping his hand and leaned his head on the passenger door, zoning out. "We'll get you home, kid."

***

The pair of Tahoes sat motionless in a roundabout outside of Power Plant Live—one of Baltimore's most well-known entertainment venues. Silten's Tahoe had suffered impact damage from the collision just outside of the Fort McHenry tunnel, which had busted a control arm on the front right tire. Meanwhile, Jeffries's Tahoe was significantly worse. Both headlights were busted, and the rear bumper had incurred extensive damage, as well as the hood and the radiator, and the front bumper was totally ripped off. Pedestrians cautiously walked by, glanced inside at the masked men, assumed the worst, and scurried away.

McDonald was hard at work, reviewing dashcam footage on his laptop for the escaped Subaru's license plate number. So far, he had come up totally empty. The chase had been a mad dash all over Baltimore, and very few moments granted a clear view of the plate.

"I'm gonna skin that bitch when we catch her," Tillman said, smiling. "Fuck taking her back for processing. She ruined my night, so she'll pay for it."

"When we catch her," Silten said, "you can do whatever the fuck you want. The kid is the only important thing. How's the plate number coming?"

"Still nothing," McDonald said. "Next time, drive in a straight line."

"Ha-fucking-ha," Silten flatly said. He pressed the transmit button on his radio. "Jeffries, how's the woman?"

The radio beeped. "Same, though she's asking to use the bathroom. Think we can at least do that? I don't wanna wash piss outta my truck."

"Negative. Give her a bottle or something. Can't risk her running off."

"Got it. We'll find something."

"Why don't we just cut our losses and go?" Peabody asked. "This kid is a hassle, and people saw us shooting at the parade."

Silten twisted around his seat to give Peabody a death stare. "Listen, discount John Candy, I saw real shit overseas in Iraq, Afghanistan, and bunch of other countries you can't even spell, so next time you think you have a bright idea, keep it to yourself. Don't think anymore. *I* do the thinking around here. We'll catch the kid and deal with that bitch and whoever the fuck was helping them."

Silten's cellphone rang. Home office. His commanding officer, Calloway.

"Fuck," Silten groaned. "I'm gonna step out to take this. Keep looking for that plate number." Silten shoved open the door and stepped out. He exhaled a deep sigh and answered the phone. "Silten here."

"Silten, what the fuck is going on out there?" Calloway yelled.

"Got a runner who's being a pesky cockroach, but we're on it."

"Really? You're on it? Because, on my laptop right now, I see video footage of a group of six agents firing into a crowd at a parade in Baltimore. The only agents in that area today were your team. Care to explain?"

"The crowd was hostile. Simple as that. People still haven't learned we're the good guys."

"You fired into an *unarmed crowd*?"

"Fired *above* an unarmed crowd."

"There's also footage of one of your men firing at an armed citizen. A Black one, too, which has certain racial implications."

"Like I said, the crowd was hostile."

"Silten, do you understand how gravity works?"

"I have a general impression, sure."

"Apparently, there was a gunshot wound near the Inner Harbor not long after your team seemed to vacate the area, but no other shooters reported. Thoughts?"

Fuck.

"If it was my team, it was an accident. Did they happen to die?"

"No, the victim is apparently gonna be fine. Just a leg wound."

"Well, then we're all good."

"No, not all good. Reports of a chase through Baltimore are circulating around here. Two Tahoes versus an Accord, and then a Subaru. Again, only your team was in the area."

"Someone's helping this kid escape. Some woman named Autumn Frost. We're handling it. We'll have this wrapped up in an hour and be back with the kid and his mom by dinner time. Then you can scratch the name *Valenz* off our search records."

Λ pause lingered on the other end of the line. "Wait," Calloway said. "Say that name again."

"Valenz. That's the name we've been looking for. Valenz."

An audible groan sounded on the other end of the line. "Oh, you fucking moron," Calloway snarled.

"*What*?"

"Your team is supposed to be picking up *Valdenz*, not *Valenz*."

Oh shit.

"Well … that certainly complicates things."

"Did you even look at the first names, or did you just go in gung-ho?"

"We were going by the intel given to us this morning."

Loud typing filled the dead air on the phone. Silten said nothing. After a few seconds, the typing stopped. "Oh, fuck me," Calloway exclaimed.

"What is it, Calloway?"

"The names given to you this morning were incorrect. It was a misprint. A typo. The AI tracking program gave you the wrong people to bring in."

"Are you fucking serious?"

"Yes, I am. And the best part is, that woman's husband is a Baltimore city councilman! Marcus Valenz! You snatched a councilman's wife, and you've been hunting her kid!"

Silten said nothing. Passersby glanced at Silten, terrified of seeing a masked man just outside their favorite music venue.

"Are you still there, Silten?"

"Yeah, I'm here."

"Release the woman and let the kid go. You're done. And after the fucking fireworks display this afternoon on Pratt Street, you'll be lucky to land a job at a gun cage. You're all finished. Get back here now and turn in your badges. You're out." The call ended.

Silten slid the phone into his pocket and watched the crowds herd toward Power Plant Live. In the back of his mind, he contemplated how many of them were legitimate Americans, and how many were illegals, faking their citizenry. How many had earned their right to be here, and how many wanted an easy ride. He wanted to punish them for taking their land, stealing their space, corrupting their peace.

All of them had to be punished.

Fuck it.

Silten slid into the driver's seat and slammed the door shut.

"Calloway?" McDonald asked.

"Yeah."

"What did he say?"

After a beat, Silten said, "Nothing important. You get it?"

"Yeah, got the license plate. Belongs to an Officer Trevor Brand, Baltimore Police."

"Oh, the police are helping her. That's cute."

"Can't seem to find the LoJack, but I managed to pull up his cellphone records. There was a call five minutes ago from the rooftop of a parking garage nearby."

Silten turned over the engine. "Then let's go huntin'."

***

Autumn and Mateo sat on the Subaru's trunk while Trevor paced around nearby. The waiting was terrible, but at least help was finally on the way. Autumn asked Trevor to message Becky that she was okay, since she still couldn't risk using her cellphone. He obliged, and Becky sent back a flurry of heart emojis.

Autumn noticed the design on Mateo's shirt. "Didn't realize you were a Judas Priest fan."

Mateo eyed the logo. "Yeah. My mom got me into them. She suggests all this old music that she used to listen to."

"Heh. Oh Lord, the fact that Judas Priest is considered old just made me age an extra ten years."

"I'm not big into modern stuff. I like the older stuff, when it was real instruments. That synth stuff seems like cheating. Learn to play an instrument or go do something else."

"You play music?"

"Learning the guitar. Started acoustic. Gonna work my way up to electric."

"Future rockstar in my presence."

Mateo chuckled, slightly embarrassed.

Autumn wrapped her arm around his shoulder and pulled him in close. "You're all right, kid. We'll get you and your mom home. Don't worry."

"Thanks, Autumn. You didn't have to help me as much as you did today. Why did you anyway?"

"It's the right thing to do. Don't need a reason."

The pair went quiet. After a moment, the trio heard screeching tires driving up the parking structure.

"All right, time to go." Autumn released Mateo and hopped off the trunk.

As she stepped forward, her smile slowly faded when a pair of black Chevy Tahoes, one severely damaged, rounded their way up the last ramp and sped forward. They parked caddy corner around the Subaru.

"What the fuck, Brand?" Autumn screamed.

"I don't know how they found us!" Trevor drew his firearm as armed masked men vacated the two vehicles and trained their sights on the trio.

Outnumbered and outgunned, Trevor, Autumn, and Mateo raised their hands.

One agent disarmed Trevor and forced him to the ground. Another agent snatched Mateo and dragged him to the rear of the first Tahoe. Mateo screamed and yelled for Autumn, who stood frozen, helpless to do anything.

No escape.

"Fuck," Autumn growled to herself.

One man, the leader, approached Autumn and removed his mask. He slicked back his hair and stared her down. "So … this bitch is Autumn Frost?"

"I'm gonna take a wild guess you're in charge."

"That's right. Name's Silten. Remember it when we cut your throat open."

"Autumn, I don't know how they found us," Trevor yelled. "Cops are on the way."

An agent kicked Trevor in the solar plexus, knocking the wind out of him.

"Stop it," Autumn screamed.

"You have made my day very difficult, Ms. Frost. And if you think you'll find your way out of this one, you've got another thing coming."

Autumn slowly cracked a smile, then chuckled.

"What's so fucking funny?" Silten asked.

"Judas Priest. I don't think they're that old."

Beyond annoyed, Silten pistol whipped Autumn across her left cheek. She fell to the ground and held her bleeding face. Then Silten sent a swift kick to her stomach, and Autumn was down for the count.

The world became hazy and dark. Weird shapes floated in her eyes. Flickering lights and dark shadows danced everywhere.

"What do we do with them?" an agent asked.

"Take 'em with us," Silten said. "I'll get the dyke. You get the nigger."

Then the world went black.

Chapter Seven

The sun was well beyond the horizon now. Baltimore's twilight had arrived. Traffic was finally flowing steadily. The city's nightlife was coming out to play. And above it, a stand-off on a random rooftop between ICE agents. The world was none the wiser.

"We're … not going back to the home office?" Peabody asked.

"No. We're to dispose of the four of them, off the books," Silten said. "The closest camp available is two hours away, and even that one is overcrowded. Home office has given us carte blanche to get rid of them however we see fit and dispose of the bodies."

"That … doesn't sound right." Peabody took a few steps backward, away from the group.

"I wouldn't expect a simpleton like you to understand, Peabody."

"Cheer up, fat boy," Tillman interrupted. "This way we all go home early. It's a nice night. Might even make it for last call."

"I–I–I–I don't like this." Peabody stepped farther away.

Arnold joined him. "Yeah, this sounds wrong. If home office said we were disposing of them, off the books, why didn't we all get a mass text to confirm? And why isn't a spot being arranged somewhere? Why do we make the decisions where they go?"

The other five agents crowded around Silten, clearly on his side. Arnold and Peabody stayed together, slowly backing up along the rooftop.

"Get in the truck. Now." Silten drew his sidearm and thumbed back the hammer.

Arnold flipped off his weapon safety. Peabody followed his lead.

"No," Arnold said. "Peabody call home office. Make sure—"

"Oh, fuck it," Tillman said. He raised his rifle and fired. Round after round ripped through Arnold and Peabody, pulverizing their faces. Tillman, a crack shot with any weapon, knew to not aim for center mass. Only headshots for a quick kill at close range.

The pair of men collapsed to the ground with chunky *thunk* sounds. Their brains spilled out of what remained of their skulls and painted the ground in dark red jelly that faded to black with the concrete.

Tillman lowered his rifle, stepped forward, and faced the group. "Well, we doing this or what? I got places to be."

Silten holstered his weapon and smirked. "You'll go far, Tillman. Yeah, we're doin' this."

"We'll need to get them somewhere out of the city," McDonald said. "County maybe?"

"Nah, that's no good. Not enough clear places to dump a body. Besides, still too close."

"Well, I'm not driving to the fucking mountains just to dump bodies. Is there a slaughterhouse nearby?" Tillman asked.

The other five agents stared at him, shocked.

"What? I'd handle it."

"I know you would, but that's too messy," Silten said. "Need somewhere more convenient. Somewhere close." Silten faced the harbor. He leaned against the edge of the roof and gazed across the city. *Where would be a good place to dispose of a body in Baltimore, where no one would find them? The harbor itself? Possibly, but harbor patrol did random dredges. Eventually they would find them. Back-alley dumpster? Easily noticeable with the heat rising in the city. Where would it be convenient to get rid of four bodies so no one would find them for weeks?*

A distant low-pitched foghorn blared. Silten snapped toward it. Across the harbor sat a massive barge docked right next to a large factory. The sign above the factory was brutally obvious—Domino Sugars. The massive glowing neon sign spilled its luscious hot-red light across Inner Harbor. Silten activated his cellphone camera and zoomed in to magnify a large crane moving scoop after scoop of raw sugar from the ship's cargo hold onto a hopper for a conveyor belt. The factory was open twenty-four hours a day, and for such a large delivery, it had to be. At that hour, though, more than likely only a night shift crew was present. Less people than normal to deal with.

Silten smiled. "Stuff Arnold and Peabody into the back of the trucks, then mount up. I know exactly where to go."

***

Stars danced in Autumn's eyes as she rejoined the waking world. She found herself lying sideways in the back of a large truck next to Mateo, who was sobbing uncontrollably. Her hands were zip tied behind her back, and all her weapons were gone. Her phone and wallet were missing too. Only her car keys remained, not that they would do her much good. She wrung her wrists, trying desperately to escape her bonds. No dice. The zip tie was pulled so tight that it nearly cut off circulation, and her hands were numb.

The truck made a wide left turn. Mateo's panicked body rolled lazily toward Autumn until the left turn ceased, then the truck drove in a straight line. He rolled back into his spot and continued his quiet sobbing.

"I'm sorry, kid. I tried," Autumn whispered.

Mateo said nothing and continued his thousand-yard stare into the truck bed.

With a jerk, the truck stopped.

Autumn heard angry yelling and screaming from two people outside. Through the muffled sounds, she could only decipher a handful of words: *believe, illegals, shutdown, step back.*

Then it went quiet.

A glowing red light blazed in through the tinted windows above Autumn's head. "Where are we?" Autumn asked no one in particular.

A scratchy voice on the other side of the seat answered. "We're at your last stop, babe. Mind if I take a bite of that taco before you go? Or maybe I could pay a visit to your chocolate factory? I like that better anyway. It would fit the location."

"You fucking pervert. Not even if you paid me."

"I ain't paying." The scratchy-voiced man turned and leered at Autumn over the edge of the backseat. "If I want a bite, I'll bite. My meat is good for that taco."

Autumn silently glared at the scratchy-voiced man. With his wiry hair and his far-too-thin face, Autumn knew immediately he wasn't lying. More than likely, he had done what he had said to others in the past.

The Tahoe's back hatch opened. A wash of red light rolled inside, illuminating Autumn and Mateo. "Out," ordered one of the ICE agents.

Mateo didn't move. His body shook, and his mind existed a thousand miles away.

"I said *out*," the agent yelled. He reached in, grabbed Mateo's shirt, and yanked him from the truck bed. The shirt ripped as he fell to the ground.

Autumn slinked her body toward the open hatch, then sat upright. She dangled her feet over the edge, then hopped to the ground. As she stood there, she examined her surroundings and spotted the Domino Sugar factory's neon sign. They were on the other side of the harbor, miles from the parking garage where ICE had captured them.

The second Tahoe's doors opened. Out poured two agents from the front and two from the back, who pulled a dead body from the center seat. It's head was wrapped in a plastic bag and hung limply from its torso. The back hatch opened, and a third body rolled onto the pavement. The head was also wrapped in plastic. As the body hit the ground, the agents reached into the back compartment and removed Trevor and Juliana. The two captives placed their feet on the ground, and an agent yanked them a few paces from the truck. Their hands were also zip tied.

Silten approached Autumn and stared down at her. He said nothing for a moment, then pointed toward a large barge docked in the harbor. "See that? That's our destination." He unsheathed a serrated combat knife and cut Autumn's bonds. He did the same to Mateo, Trevor, and Juliana, then faced Autumn. "Pick up the bodies and let's go."

"Where the fuck is everyone? There are cameras everywhere," Trevor said.

"Gone, baby. Everyone is long gone," said the wiry agent gleefully. "We told them that we were stopping by for a random inspection. They skedaddled not a second later. And McDonald here disabled the camera system. We got the place all to ourselves. Guess we'll have to make a return trip, won't we, boys?"

"Shut it," Silten yelled. "Frost, you and the kid get that one." He pointed toward a stocky-looking dead agent. Then he faced Trevor and Juliana. "And, you two, get that one." He pointed toward a fat agent. "Move it."

Autumn and Mateo hefted the stocky guy, with Autumn at the head, Mateo at the feet. Trevor and Juliana did the same for the fat one, with Trevor at the head, Juliana at the feet. The four captives strained to carry such heavy loads. Juliana became exhausted quickly, and Trevor struggled with his injured shoulder. As they trudged toward the docked boat, the ICE agents traipsed behind them, weapons at the ready. Even without telling her, Autumn knew exactly what would happen once they reached the ship. The agents would shoot them and bury all six bodies deep into the cargo hold. They wouldn't be found for weeks, possibly not even while still in Baltimore. The ship might leave port for its next destination, and they'd be found seven states away.

If you're gonna do something, Autumn thought, *do it now*.

Autumn eyed the heavy body dangling from her hands and noticed, on his chest, a bunch of spare magazines for an assault rifle that was long since gone, but she also saw her one get-out-of-jail-free card: a flashbang grenade.

One chance. Don't fuck it up, Frost.

"Hang on, hang on," Autumn wheezed.

"What is it?" Silten asked.

Autumn dropped the stocky agent to the ground. She doubled over and leaned on her knees. "This guy is too heavy for the kid. See how he's struggling? It'll be faster without him."

When Mateo raised a brow at Autumn, she shot back a quick wink.

"I'm not having any of my men carrying this dead weight," Silten said.

Autumn pushed herself off her knees and rose. "They won't have to. I can carry him by myself."

"Really? You?"

"Yeah, me. Do I look small to you? One on one, I could level any of you fucking Nazis."

"You watch your fucking mouth, twat." Silten examined her. She was certainly built tough. Muscles everywhere, huge quads, which meant a sturdy gait, and biceps that could crush bricks. "Fine. You carry him. Get on with it."

Autumn kneeled and rolled the stocky agent onto her back. Then she heaved him up with Herculean effort until his waistline rested upon her right shoulder. He was heavy but nothing she couldn't handle.

And next to her right ear was the flashbang grenade.

"Oh, and Frost," the wiry man said.

Autumn turned and leered at the man.

Grinning, the man said, "*Sieg heil*, bitch."

Autumn spit at his feet, turned around, and put one foot in front of the other.

The group moved once again in a death march toward the ship. Autumn pulled ahead of the entire group, grunting with each step, until she could find the right moment to make her play. Mateo marched alongside Autumn. She slowed a bit to allow Trevor to catch up. Once he did, she shot him an intense, focused expression that said *Get ready*. Trevor noticed the ring of the flashbang grenade dangling next to Autumn's ear and got the message loud and clear.

As they passed a pair of metal shipping containers, Autumn figured that would be the best chance. The containers were spaced a few feet apart, creating narrow metal canyons. Large overhead spotlights shone into the cargo hold. The illumination blanketed the entire port and lit the side of the sugar factory facing the ship. Hiding in the factory would be their best chance.

Now or never.

Autumn slowly raised her left hand.

Trevor cast quick glances to his right as she got ready.

She slid her finger through the ring on the grenade.

Mateo watched her, mentally preparing himself to run.

Autumn smirked and ripped out the pin. She heaved the body behind her at the ICE agents and pulled Mateo to the ground. "*Duck!*"

Trevor dropped the agent and leaped at Juliana to knock her to the ground.

The agents stopped, confused. The wiry man said, "What the f—!"

BANG!

A brilliant, blinding flash of light and a thundercrack explosion were all it took to disable six ICE agents. They stumbled around, screaming and swearing, lost in a blurry world of white light. Silten was especially angry and letting it all out. "*You fuck! You fuck, Frost!*"

Autumn and Trevor snapped into action. They dragged Mateo and Juliana to their feet and followed behind Autumn. They bolted through the columns of shipping containers and darted into the next column. Once the canyon of containers ended, the group grinded to a halt. Autumn looked to her right at an entrance door in the shadows of the shipping containers. She grasped the handle and pulled.

Locked.

She jangled the handle and pulled harder. It didn't budge.

Pumped with adrenaline and rage, she grasped the door handle with both hands and pulled with the force of rabid animal. Gritting her teeth and snarling like a beast, she pulled and pulled, muscles rippling as she gave it everything she had. She placed her foot on the wall next to the latch to gain extra leverage. Finally, the latch gave way, and the door flung wide open. Autumn swayed with the door for a second, shocked by her own strength.

Trevor, aghast, said, "Goddamn."

"Oh, jerk off to me later," Autumn groaned. "Come on! Get in!"

Trevor, Mateo, and Juliana rushed inside the bright interior.

Through the containers, yelling and screaming echoed. Someone, probably Silten, screamed, "*You're fucking dead, Frost! There's no way out! You're fucking dead, you dyke bitch!*"

Steeling herself, she crossed the threshold into the factory.

Chapter Eight

Over one hundred years old, the Baltimore Domino Sugar factory was a landmark of local pride. It shipped more than ninety million pounds of raw sugar daily to the port, refined into various forms—white, brown, raw, and even powdered. It was an extensive process that had become one of the prime economic sources for the city and employed over five hundred people. And while the factory had received the occasional upgrade and facelift since its construction, the basic nuts and bolts of production remained generally the same.

Now, though, all the factory workers had run off, and the port was a ghost town, except for four innocent people on the run from six ICE agents.

Autumn and Trevor lead the way down a dusty corridor. Juliana and Mateo followed close behind. To their left were massive round silver vats with cone-shaped tops and pipes leading upward into the ceiling. To their right was a conveyor belt loaded with cardboard Domino–branded boxes of processed sugar, ready for delivery. Above the belt was a long row of dispenser cones for depositing sugar into every box.

The factory smelled bittersweet—a pungent smell of burning sugar.

At the end of the row of silver vats, Trevor saw a control panel for the conveyor belt. He dashed toward it and flipped on the power. The conveyor moved once again, and the overhead cones dropped squirts of sugar into boxes flowing along the belt. A monotonous *reee-deeesssh-reee* echoed in the room as box after box moved down the belt.

"What the hell are you doing?" Autumn asked.

"The sound. Keep it loud so they can't track us," Trevor stated. "Let's go."

They continued around the next corner, where they found themselves in a raw-sugar processing room. A long row of centrifuges populated the left side of the room. Above the centrifuges were a series of metal pipes running across the ceiling. They jutted downward and hung directly over the centrifuges to deposit their streams of sugar. The ceiling resembled the back of a porcupine, with the number of pipes leading to and from every location. On the right stretched a seemingly endless row of four-foot-high basins filled with thick molasses. It boiled and bubbled as it slowly churned clockwise.

"Where the fuck do we hide?" Autumn yelled.

"Main office," Trevor said. "Gotta be a phone."

The group darted forward, rounding corner after corner, venturing deeper into unknown territory. Everything looked the same. No matter their location, it seemed to be the same rough-looking pipes, girders, vats, belts, cages, and boxes. How anyone made it through the place without a map was beyond Autumn.

As they entered another row of cooking vats, she spotted a large red pipe wrench on a tool rack. With all her weapons gone, she would take what she could get. She snatched it up and kept moving.

They darted around another corner and came face-to-face with the muzzle end of a rifle and two ICE agents. Due to the noise, both groups surprised each other. Autumn dashed into action and swung hard upward at the first agent who had a long goatee. The wrench connected with the bottom of his rifle muzzle, knocking it upward. The gun sprayed a burst into a vat of boiling sugar. The hot liquid sprayed and doused the second agent with molten sugar. He screamed in pain and collapsed to the floor, cradling his masked face, as the flesh slowly melted from the bone and became encrusted to the mask.

Autumn took the initiative and attacked again. She jabbed hard at the goatee agent's trachea. He recoiled and grasped his windpipe. With one massive swoop, she reeled back and swung downward, cracking the agent across the right side of his head. He crashed to the floor, his brain slowly seeping from the fracture in his skull.

Upon seeing the brains, Juliana retched in horror.

Trevor kneeled. He snatched the rifle and another flashbang, the latter of which he handed to Autumn. Before he could grab the rest of the agent's kit, gunfire surrounded them. Down the corridor, the remaining four agents trained their rifles and released burst after burst of gunfire. The four retreated the way they had come and took the first right they could. This led to a four-way intersection. To the left was a series of offices for filing reports and business meetings. Straight ahead was more hallways of pipes and vats that led who-knew-where. And to the right was a section specifically for powdered sugar processing.

"Split up. Go to the offices and find a phone," Autumn directed. "I'll handle them."

"Here, take this." Trevor proffered the rifle.

"No, you need that to protect them. I'll figure it out."

"What the fuck are you gonna do?"

Autumn spotted a caution sign that read NO SMOKING. CONTENTS EXPLOSIVE. Underneath the caution sign hung a picture of powdered sugar.

"Go out with a bang, maybe. Get to a phone. Get the cops here. I'll handle this."

Trevor, Mateo, and Juliana rushed toward the offices. Autumn stood her ground in the center of the intersection. Given the circumstances, most people would consider the chain of events that led to that moment. What had they done to deserve this? Did this mean anything? Was all this worth dying for? Autumn Frost, however, didn't consider any of these thoughts. All she thought to herself was *Don't need a reason to do the right thing.*

Silten and company rounded the corner and spotted Autumn, waiting.

The buff redhead raised the bloody, brain-soaked wrench and pointed it at Silten. "You want me? I'm right here … *Nazi.*" Then she bolted to the right toward the massive processing section, with four-by-three rows of ten-meter-high cylindrical vats, all churning and burning. An incessant humming noise charged the space with energy as Autumn dashed between the vats to seek cover. Above the vats was a catwalk that spanned the length of the room, with several offshoots overlooking each row. A thin staircase at the opposite end of the room led to the catwalk.

As Autumn took cover behind a cylinder, she noticed a reflective surface on the vat opposite her. Though distorted and blurry, she could see the length of the room. Through the distortion, she noticed an agent walking down the pathway. She looked to her opposite side and saw another agent doing the same. One agent per path. They were canvasing the room. And eventually, they would find her.

Sighing, Autumn leaned back and considered her options, which were already slim to none. She chastised herself, whispering, "Stupid, stupid, stupid." As she leaned against the vat, the edge of the flashbang dug into her side.

No Smoking. Contents explosive.

She snapped her head upward and saw the catwalks crisscrossing over the vats. *Fuck it, be bold.*

***

Silten kept his weapon at the ready as he inched down the pathway, knowing she was waiting for them, intent on springing some trap. She wouldn't catch him, though. He was ready and prepared. A full magazine was loaded into his rifle, and every round had Autumn Frost's name etched on them.

To his right, in the next two pathways, Tillman and Jeffries kept pace, scanning for their prey. Silten had ordered Caldwell to go after the cop and the illegals.

Three ex-military versus a TAF driver? Easy.

A redheaded blur bolted across Tillman's row. Tillman fired. No joy.

"Sound off," Silten screamed.

"She's here," Tillman yelled over the humming vats. "That fucking bitch is here!"

"Frost! Come on out, and we'll make it quick!"

"Eat my ass, you bottom boy bitch," Autumn screamed from somewhere. The echo traveled between the vats. It was impossible to pinpoint her location.

A loud clang sounded, and a valve on a vat exploded, shooting hot steam into one of the pathways.

Another redheaded blur across the vats. Tillman fired again. Another miss.

Clang! Another valve exploded. More hot steam.

"Oh. Clever," Silten said to himself. *Can't go through the steam. But what the fuck are you planning, Frost?*

"You see her?" Jeffries screamed. The noise was deafening in the room.

"No," Tillman replied.

"Where the fuck is she?"

"Oh, boys," a feminine voice above shouted.

Silten, Tillman, and Jeffries looked up at the catwalk, where Autumn Frost stood next to the vat closest to an office door. They trained their rifles on her.

"Fun fact about powdered sugar." Autumn unhitched a flashbang grenade from her hip and pulled the pin. "It's flammable." She casually chucked it over the edge of the railing, and it landed smack dab inside a sugar vat.

"*No*," screamed all three agents.

Autumn dashed into the office and dove for the floor.

A glorious, thunderous eruption blasted through the room. The shockwave rippled through everything and destroyed vat after vat. The windows exploded, shooting shards of glass all over the concrete outside. A brilliant white fireball surged toward the roof and filled the room with thick sweet smoke.

The blast sent Jeffries backward toward a metal railing. His head slammed into the middle rail, splitting open the back of his skull, killing him instantly. Tillman took the brunt of the explosion and shot clear across the center pathway to the opposite end of the room. He rammed into the wall, broke four ribs, and suffered a concussion.

Silten had taken cover at the last second behind a palette of metal piping, though it only protected him from the main explosion. Hot molten sugar sprayed from the first vat, like an erupting volcano, and doused his entire body. Molten brown liquid coated his facemask, chest, and pants. Screaming, he ripped off his Kevlar vest, mask, and pants. Everything burned. As he scratched away the remnants of molten fluid, bits of his skin and muscle tissue peeled away. Pulling, tugging, tearing, it was excruciating. Once it was all gone, he gazed at his face in the reflection of one of the vats. The teeth in his right-side jawline were exposed, and cheek bones were visible. Blood trickled out, and his undershirt reddened.

With psychotic fury, Silten screamed out, *"FROOOOOOOSSSSSTTTTTT!!!!"*

***

"Get here as fast as you can," Trevor said. "They're coming for us." He slammed the phone on its receiver and approached the mother and her son.

Juliana and Mateo scrambled to open a window that led to a fire escape. The office was part of the cubicle barnyard for shipping and receiving. A large meeting room, with an elongated table, was farther down the hallway, though there was no cover. Thankfully, the power was still on. Harsh, artificial lights soaked the room. Every cubicle was the same save for personal items—flat-screen computers, rolling office chairs, five-foot-high walls coated with foam for soundproofing. It was dull and uninspired, not unlike Trevor's own police precinct across town.

"Let me try," Trevor said to Juliana and Mateo. He flipped his rifle around and smashed out the window. It shattered and rained shards onto the concrete below.

Mateo mounted the windowsill and carefully crossed through. Just as he put his feet onto the iron grating of the fire escape, a hail of gunfire erupted around Juliana and Trevor. Mateo ducked below the windowsill for cover.

Two rounds penetrated Trevor's right forearm. He and Juliana ducked and took cover in a cubicle. The gunfire ceased, leaving only a pregnant silence. Elsewhere in the factory, Trevor heard hollow gunfire. Somewhere, Autumn was keeping the rest of the agents busy. Between the shots, Trevor heard soft footsteps slowly creeping between the cubicles, searching for them.

"You know, this afternoon, I shot at cops in the tunnel," the creeping voice said. "I'd like to say that was a first, but it wasn't."

Trevor covered Juliana's mouth to stifle her panting. They sat with their backs against the cubicle wall, the rifle aimed upward at the opening, waiting for the perfect moment to fire. With only one-half-good arm remaining, Trevor would get one shot, and nothing more.

"I've lost track of how many of you pigs I've put down. There's always a few of you who just don't get that we're the good guys. Well, what's one more?"

Shuffling nearby. The agent's shadow stopped just short of the cubicle entrance. Then came a light *ka-chink* sound. Trevor had heard that sound before—the pin of a flashbang being pulled.

"So, come on out, pig. I'll make—"

An enormous explosion blasted through the offices, shredding the tops of the cubicles. Office supplies flew everywhere and tore apart the room.

The ICE agent fell forward just outside the opening of the cubicle and landed on the armed flashbang grenade. "No, no—!" The blast went off directly under his chest, stifling the sound. An eruption of blood and gore sprayed outward, dousing Trevor and Juliana.

Fighting through the pain, Trevor stood and used his foot to roll the agent onto his back. His chest cavity was split wide open. Despite his injuries, the agent continued breathing, shallow and wheezy. Trevor considered firing a mercy shot but decided against it. Instead, he stared at the near-dead agent and proudly said, "You know, on behalf of every pig in Baltimore, I hope that hurts. A lot."

A few gurgles later, the agent stopped breathing.

A gore-covered Juliana sprang to her feet and rushed to the broken window. She looked over the edge. No Mateo. "Mateo? *Mateo*?"

***

The scared kid rushed down the fire escape. Step after step felt like he was a little closer to freedom. As he reached the last set of stairs, an explosion rocked the building. He fell end over end and landed back-first on the concrete below, which punched the wind out of him. He shakily rose to his feet and heard a second small explosion in the office above. He considered going back up, but he had no idea if that last explosion meant his mother was safe or dead. With no options left, Mateo trudged toward the factory exit.

Bang! Gunfire erupted around him. Silten, far in the distance, shakily aimed a rifle in Mateo's direction. He was half naked, and his body looked half melted. *Bang bang bang!* Mateo darted toward the shipping containers. Silten gave chase and chucked away the empty rifle.

Mateo searched for somewhere to run. The trucks were too far to make a clean escape. The factory was destroyed and on fire. He looked right at the docked boat. Summoning his last bit of courage, Mateo dashed toward the jetty leading to the boat deck.

Silten opened fire with his sidearm. The rounds pinged off the jetty.

Mateo halted in his tracks. Fueled by instinct and adrenaline, he climbed the stairway to his left. More gunfire pinged off the railing surrounding the steps. Once he was halfway up, Mateo realized his error. The stairs led to the crane.

A dead end.

Mateo looked down at a half-skull-faced Silten climbing after him.

With no choice left, he climbed.

***

There was three of everything when Tillman rose to his feet. The wall behind him had collapsed, exposing the artificially lit outside world. He swayed and shuffled around, unsure of where he was. His concussion impaired his sense of sight, hearing, and smell.

Then a brutal crunch of a pipe wrench snapped the bones in his right arm.

He yelped in pain. *What's happening?!*

Another swipe, this time across his left cheek. Four teeth shattered instantly, and blood ejaculated from his mouth.

Then another downward swipe across the left cheek. The wrench hit his jaw and ripped it from the hinge joint. His jaw fell limp, and blood poured from the fresh wound.

Tillman dropped to his knees, confused and terrified. "Ma jer. Yu bruk ma jer!"

A red flaming shape leaned into his view. Through muffled sound, he heard a voice say, "Your meat couldn't handle this taco!"

The flaming red shape reeled itself upward, like the wings of a large bird getting ready for flight. As he gazed up, he had one final thought. *Oh. Pretty.*

Then a final blow descended upon him and penetrated deep into his skull with a mushy crunch.

***

Autumn relaxed and stared down at Tillman. He was stone dead but still kneeled upright, a waterfall of blood pouring from his brain and jawline. Eyes open but lifeless. It had been a long time since she'd felt such satisfaction.

Smoke was filling the room inside the factory. Autumn grasped the blood-soaked pipe wrench embedded in Tillman's skull. She cantilevered it to the opposite side and yanked it out. It gave off a wet, crunchy sound, like someone ripping open a cantaloupe.

Finally, Tillman toppled over, and his brain matter spilled onto the floor.

Autumn leaped over a knee-high section of what remained of the wall and dashed outside. She breathed deep. Fresh air once again.

Then, gunshots.

She snapped left and saw Silten popping off shots toward someone climbing the stairs to the crane. *Mateo.*

"Ugh, fucking figures," she groaned. Though exhausted, torn up, and all-around pissed off, Autumn dug deep for whatever she had left and sprinted for the crane.

Chapter Nine

The crane above the boat was known as a hammerhead due to its obvious hammer-shaped design. It was a workhorse of dockyards and featured a horizontal cabling system for loading and unloading cargo. On the back end was a small cramped sheet metal cabin designed for manual control, and beyond the cabin was a fifty-foot gantry that extended over the boat.

Mateo burst into the cabin and searched for anywhere to hide. It was far too small, and no space was suitable to squeeze into. No tools for defense either.

"You little spic fuck," Silten screamed. "Stay still, and I'll end you fast."

Mateo snapped around at Silten trudging into the cabin, half naked, half melted, and brandishing his serrated combat knife—the stuff of nightmares.

Terrified, Mateo shoved open the gantry door, dashed through, and slammed it closed behind him. He ran to the end of the gantry and looked over the edge at the hundred-foot drop to the deck. The cargo hold was still open, exposing an enormous mound of brown raw sugar to the world. Just below the end of the gantry, the crane scoop dangled, still loaded with sugar.

"Turn around, you fucking kid," Silten growled.

Mateo slowly turned toward the murderous agent standing less than fifteen feet away, half smiling with what remained of his jaw. With nowhere to go, he cried out, "Oh God. Mom, where are you?"

"Hey, asshole," a woman's voice called out.

Silten spun and saw his mutilator—Autumn Frost.

"Goddamn, Silten," Autumn said. "I wish I had a camera 'cause this image is just too good."

"You fucking bitch," Silten screamed. "Don't go anywhere! You're next!"

"Or how about me first?" She lifted her bloody pipe wrench and tapped it into her opposite hand, ready to fight. "No one left but us."

Snarling, Silten snapped toward Mateo. "Get to you in a second." He faced Autumn. "You don't even know this fucking kid! He's not special, he's not important, and he's not one of us! He and all his fucking kind shouldn't be here! What the fuck do you even matter either? You're just some TAF driver and a fucking dyke too!"

A gentle wind blustered. Wisps of smoke from the factory drifted around the crane and floated toward the city beyond.

Autumn swiped her hair from her eyes. "You gonna whine all night, Nazi Skeletor ... or are you gonna fight this dyke bitch?"

Silten charged forward and slashed at Autumn. A clear miss; a scare tactic. Autumn recoiled and brought her wrench to bear. Silten bent his knees and raised his blade, waiting for Autumn to make a move.

Autumn dashed forward, swinging upward at Silten's chin. A near miss that rendered Silten off balance. He stumbled backward, regained his footing, and charged forward with a flurry of slashes. One connected with Autumn's stomach. Her shirt ripped, and blood flowed. A superficial slice, though painful, nonetheless.

Autumn steadied herself and considered her options. She remembered her boxing lessons. Wait for the opponent to get impatient and make a mistake, then exploit it and abuse it. She raised her wrench at Silten and tilted it twice toward herself. An obvious taunt. *Come get me, punk.*

Silten charged again, stabbing forward. Autumn darted left, grabbed his arm, and swung the wrench downward at Silten's hand. Two fingers broke, and the knife clattered onto the gantry. As Silten stumbled backward, Autumn kneeled and grabbed the knife. She stared at Silten, smirked, then chucked the knife over the edge of the gantry. It gave off a sharp clatter as it crashed to the ground below.

"What else you got?" Autumn asked.

Burning with fury, Silten rushed forward, dodged Autumn's attack, and piledrove into her. The pair crashed to the gantry and grappled with each other. Autumn's wrench clattered to the deck behind her. Silten mounted Autumn around her waist and threw a one-two punch—one across the left check, one across the right cheek. As a third punch descended, Autumn spit a geyser of blood into Silten's eyes. He recoiled, lost in a sea of red.

Autumn stretched above her as much as she could for her wrench. Silten clasped her throat and dragged her to her feet. With him crushing her windpipe, Autumn felt herself fading.

"You know, you dykes don't even have half of what we do," Silten snarled.

Come on, Autumn! Do something! Anything! "You know, you're right," Autumn croaked out. "There is one thing you guys have that we don't."

"What's that?"

Autumn fumbled her car keys from her pocket and shot mace into Silten's eyes. He released Autumn and recoiled, blinded. She ran down the gantry, retrieved her wrench, and swung hard upward into Silten's balls. He released a high-pitched scream as both his testicles exploded.

"Weak points," she roughly answered. Autumn smiled, reeled back, and swung a hard right hook with her wrench, knocking Silten over the edge of the gantry railing.

He toppled over, fell a few feet, and, at the last second, grabbed hold of the crane scoop.

"Oh, for fuck's sake." Autumn crossed over the railing and hopped atop the scoop.

Silten said nothing but pleaded with his reddened eyes.

A wave of anger rushed through Autumn as she swung toward Silten's hands, screaming with each swing. "*YOU! FUCKED! UP! MY! CAR!*"

One last swing, and the wrench smashed Silten's hand into paste. The agent fell, screaming, toward the cargo hold, a hundred feet down. He landed feet first on the massive pile of sugar. His kneecaps exploded, and the bones in his lower legs shattered. A surge of blood and gore burst forth and coated the once-brown sugar with red velvet.

"Eww," Autumn groaned. She chucked the wrench away. It clattered loudly as it hit the ship's deck below. Exhausted, she turned and began climbing to the gantry. Totally gassed, she couldn't make it.

Then a hand reached down to her. "Come on," Mateo said.

Autumn smiled and grabbed ahold. Once she was back up top, Autumn lay flat on the gantry deck, staring into the night sky.

Mateo sat next to her and leaned against the railing. "Thanks, Autumn."

"Don't mention it," she responded weakly.

Together they leaned over the edge of the gantry and gazed at the fallen agent. Despite all his injuries, he still moved.

Shocked, Autumn said, "The fuck? Is he still alive?"

On ground level, Juliana located an emergency control box at the base of the crane. She unlatched the box and snapped it open. Inside was a button labeled EMERGENCY LOAD RELEASE. She reached out and growled, "*Hijo de puta.*" Then she pressed the button.

Just below the gantry, the scoop released and fell toward the open cargo hold below.

As the ten-ton scoop crashed toward him, Silten screamed out a guttural, "*NOOOOOOOOOO*—" Then it crushed him into liquid.

As the dust settled, Autumn shrugged. "Oh. Never mind."

***

A police helicopter circled the now-destroyed factory. Its spotlight shone into what used to be the processing section. The fires were mostly extinguished, and EMS, firefighters, and police were on the scene to canvas the area.

Trevor Brand, covered in bandages, bruises, and with one arm in a sling, was on the phone with the head of DHS, while Autumn, Mateo, and Juliana sat on the back bumper of an ambulance, receiving medical care. As Trevor finished his call, a black Lincoln Town Car drove onto the lot, with Marcus Valenz as the passenger. Mateo and Juliana sprang up and rushed toward him. Marcus opened his arms and lovingly embraced his family. Autumn watched from a distance and smiled.

Seeking to make a good impression, Trevor introduced himself to Marcus. Autumn watched but couldn't hear what they said.

After a few moments, Trevor excused himself and approached Autumn. "Just got off the phone with DHS."

"*Ohhhh*, here it comes," Autumn said.

The EMS tech poked something at the cut on Autumn's stomach.

Annoyed, she shouted, "Hey, could you stop, please? I'm fine."

The tech backed off and walked away.

Trevor sat to Autumn's left to inspect where Silten had pistol whipped her earlier. "Damn, you're gonna need some serious makeup for that. It's gonna turn black and blue in no time."

"Call it a battle scar. Anyway, you were saying?"

"Seems Silten's team was off book and had been told to release the Valenzes. But they went AWOL, and here we are."

"And because they were AWOL, DHS claims no responsibility, ICE is never reprimanded, and no one up top gets punished."

Trevor shrugged. "It's almost like you're a psychic."

"No, it's almost like I'm a cynic."

The pair went silent and watched the controlled chaos before them. Overhead, the helicopter flew away, and the sound of rotor blades slowly faded.

Autumn sighed. "Even when we win, we lose."

"Life in America," Trevor said.

"*Yuuuup.*"

"But, hey"—Trevor pointed toward the Valenzes—"You saved them, at least."

"Yeah, my good deed for the day. And as punishment for my good deed, I have a broken-down car, probably two dozen traffic violations, and I just blew up one of the most well-known landmarks in all of Baltimore."

"Well, if it makes you feel any better, I can probably get the traffic violations stricken from your record."

"*Thaaaannnkkkkks* a million."

Trevor chuckled and pulled a foil-wrapped phone from his pocket. "Oh, an officer found this in one of the agent's pockets." He handed it to Autumn.

She unwrapped the foil and noticed a long hairline crack ran right down the middle of the phone's screen.

"Sorry, it's cracked," Trevor added.

Autumn shook her head, sighed, and set it beside her. "Every good thing in my life has a caveat."

"You know, I got a question."

"I probably have an answer."

"Why did you help them today? No one else would have done what you did."

After a beat, Autumn replied, "Didn't really have anywhere else to be today."

Trevor scoffed and shook his head.

Autumn chuckled.

"Get outta here, Frosty. I'll clean this up. We'll call you when we need you for a statement."

Autumn smirked at Trevor.

"Go, Frost. Before I change my mind. Go."

Autumn snatched her phone, stood, and faced Trevor. "You know, for a pig …" Autumn smacked Trevor's injured shoulder.

Trevor gave off a long, painful groan.

"… you ain't half bad." Then she walked away.

"Hey, everyone loves the smell of bacon in the morning," Trevor shouted.

Autumn turned and shot Trevor the middle finger as she walked backward.

He returned the gesture, smiling.

As Autumn maneuvered around hordes of people toward the Valenzes, a security detail stopped her and held her back.

"No, it's okay," Marcus said.

The security released Autumn and allowed her to pass.

"Ms. Frost, thank you so much for today. From the bottom of my heart, I can't thank you enough."

"Well, I'm happy to help," she half-lied.

"I've never seen someone fight like you," Juliana said. "I'm so grateful that Mateo ended up in your car."

"Seems to be a weird occurrence with me these days," Autumn said.

"*Hmmm?*"

"Never mind. Just glad you guys are safe. You especially, kid. Gonna have to get you a new shirt now. You like Ozzy?"

"Who doesn't?" Mateo answered.

Autumn smiled. "That's the spirit."

"Is there *anything* I can do for you, Ms. Frost? Do you need a ride home?" Marcus asked.

A ride. "Actually, there is one thing. My car is kinda fucked and is over on the other side of the harbor. If you guys could somehow reimburse me and get it fixed, I'd appreciate it."

"I will make sure it happens."

Autumn secretly activated her phone's video recorder and casually aimed it at Marcus. "You're sure? You can get my car fixed up?"

"I just said I will make it happen."

"You will reimburse me and get my car fixed up?"

"Yes, Ms. Frost! Why do you keep asking?"

"Well, see, I needed the video footage of you saying that on camera so I have insurance in case you try to dick me over."

Marcus's once candid demeanor melted into aggravation and annoyance.

"Hey, you're a politician in Baltimore," Autumn stated. "You think I'm stupid?"

Suppressing his anger, Marcus cleared his throat. "No, Ms. Frost. I do not think you're stupid."

"Great! With that done, I'm going home." Autumn patted Mateo's shoulder. "Good luck, kid. Don't do anything I would do."

Autumn turned and headed for the front gate. She opened her phone and called Becky, who answered on the first ring.

"Autumn, are you okay?" Becky asked, panicking.

"I'm okay, babe. Still in Baltimore. Let's just say things overall worked out. And hey, I know you worked all day, but my car is screwed. Could you come pick me up?"

"Of course. Where are you?"

"I'll pin my location once I get back to my car. See you soon, babe. Love ya."

Autumn ended the call and checked the distance to the garage where she'd dumped her Accord. Over a forty-minute walk. "Fuck that," she whispered. She opened the TAF app and ordered a driver for herself.

Ten minutes later, Autumn walked into the garage where her car was parked. She rounded a corner and spotted it exactly where she had left it. The slight smell of gasoline still lingered in the air. The remains of Becky's calamari were strewn across the ground. Autumn shook her head in frustration.

With nothing else to do, she walked down to Pratt Street. The roadway was completely different from the afternoon—no parade, no music, just another street in Baltimore, like nothing had happened all day.

She turned left and entered Pratt Street Ale House. The place was half-full and loud with music and chatter. Golden light bounced everywhere, and the smell of beer and fried food filled the air. As Autumn approached the bar, several people noticed her blood-covered shirt, filthy hands, and bruised face. The music slowly lowered, and people stared.

Autumn said nothing and sat at the bar.

The bartender eyed Autumn, shocked by her appearance. "*Umm*, are you okay?"

"Aces. Could I have a glass of water please?"

The bartender filled a glass and handed it to Autumn. She chugged it down in one go, slammed the glass onto the bar top, and breathed deep.

"*Umm*, would you like a drink-drink too?"

After a moment, Autumn replied, "Yeah. Whiskey. Neat. Because fuck ICE."

About the Author

Born in the suburbs of Maryland in 1985, Jesse Fresco began writing as an escape from his day job as a stagehand. His work is heavily inspired by his sixteen years in the film industry and various life experiences. An avid reader with a library of over four hundred prose novels and graphic novels, he found inspiration in the works of Garth Ennis, Lee Child, Derek Robinson, and Stephen King. He currently lives in Davidsonville, Maryland with his family.

To get in contact with the author, go to
http://www.instagram.com/jessefresco
https://www.facebook.com/jessefresco
https://www.threads.com/@jessefresco
https://x.com/HardCoreBShot